Southern Prejudice
& Injustice

By:

June Poore

Cover illustration by:
June Poore

Nine Lives Publishing
Knoxville, TN

In loving dedication to my *Mother;*

She reared me to love a good, simple story.

She taught me that life will give you all that you need;

To always look before you leap; and if you fall off of that bull known as life, get back on and grab it by the horns and ride it for all its worth!

Appropriately, this book of three, simple, short stories is

All about life and the bull. (And bullying.)

Contents:

Acknowledgements:

I want to thank my mother, who gifted me the talent of writing which came through her creative DNA and genes.

I want to thank my God, because He created me, gave me a chance at life and made me who I am today.

Southern Prejudice

& Injustice

Preface:

These three short stories had to be written. For many years they have demanded to be put to print. Stirring around inside of my brain, words forming and rearranging as they mustered a life of their own. You see, all three stories are based on someone I knew, or someone related to me. Although written from a fictional standpoint, all three tales are based on real life people and events.

Names, locations and/or events have been altered to protect the innocent.

Too bad that I had to protect the "not so innocent" antagonists who made these tales so important to write. Because it is the "**bully**", the "**hater**", and the "**persecutor**" *who makes our lives much more difficult than is necessary.*

This book is written for all of the people who have faced prejudice, injustice, racism, bigotry and bias.

The Hermit

Feb 3, 2018

Written by T.R. Love & J. Poore

Cultural clashes, and lack of understanding has driven many a wedge between man and his own kind. That which drives one man forward can drive another man far, far away.

When Richard left North Carolina, he traveled through many areas, searching for something he knew he would recognize when he found it. The something he craved most was peace. He had never known peace his entire life, and Richard wasn't exactly a young man anymore. His travels took him across many hundreds of miles, this is how he discovered the Appalachian mountains of East Tennessee. He was a wise Native-American from an Indian reservation in Cherokee, NC. Wise enough to recognize the potential of the land he had stumbled upon.

Richard was a determined man, with all of his worldly belongings strapped to his back and on the backs of his horses along with the two women who traveled with him. His companions were his wife Pearl, and sister n law Dawn, they were seeking a new life with privacy, good land which would yield crops, with enough acreage to allow them to build easily with plenty of room to grow. They found such a location after a long journey, the three of them preparing to settle down on the outskirts of a coal mining camp. They were excited to make their new life in the hills of East Tennessee.

During these times in the early 1900's, in the mountainous Appalachian region, it wasn't uncommon for inhabitants to discover unused land, and to take it over. It was recognized then as *squatter's rights*, basically, if you claimed a vacant piece of land, cleared it and made good use of it with no dispute, it belonged to you. This is how Richard and his family acquired secluded acreage atop a hill, where he used his survival skills to build their home. Pearl and Dawn were very capable of helping him, as both women were at their peak physically.

Arriving during early spring afforded them many benefits, namely longer days which provided natural light for their hard work. Most days weren't too hot during the spring season, and when it didn't rain the family worked together from daylight until dusk. Right away it was clear to the other families who lived in the settlement that these three "strangers" were close-knit, and somewhat hesitant to make friends. Not once did the "Indians", as they were called, ever ask for help. By the same token, not once did anyone *offer* help.

The three Native Americans made most of the tools they needed, such as hammers, picks and shovels, primitive saws and chisels. Richard was very handy and determined, he knew he had to have a shelter in place before the cold winter came. There were plenty of trees for him to chop down to use the wood to build a small log cabin, known then as a "shotgun cabin", which was a small, rectangular dwelling, a simple structure with a fireplace for cooking and warming the cabin. He made two wooden beds with wooden slats to hold a bag of straw and dried leaves for he and Pearl to sleep on, he made a smaller one for Dawn.

Although their dwelling was complete by the first cold spell of winter, Richard still had years of work ahead of him to make his cabin atop the hill into a real home. They would require a large garden from which they could eat, and the earth had to be fertile to yield such crops. But the hard work was satisfying and brought hope of a better future where he and Pearl planned to eventually raise a family. Their dream was to be free and live in one place where no one could take their home or freedom away from them.

Before he was even born his ancestors had moved from their territory and fought wars with the "white man" just to live in peace. Around 1838 history tells us that the Cherokee resisted effort to move and was forced to make the long trip to new territory. Refusing to give up, the Indian nations continued their march, losing men, women and children along the way due to disease, exposure and starvation. Tens of thousands were driven from their homes by federal soldiers. Their journey was remembered as the *Trail of Tears*. Even though this occurred long before Richard's birth, many families remained unsettled for decades afterwards in search of a permanent place to rebuild and to flourish. As well, families and tribes were divided, and many families went their separate ways. This had been the case with Richard.

He had lost his parents at a rather young age and teamed up working for Pearl's father, until her father's untimely demise. It was then that Richard joined Pearl's mother and her two daughters on a journey of peace. But peace had been difficult to find. Pearl's mother had died a year earlier to disease. Richard and her daughters left North Carolina, solemnly swearing to never return. Traveling from place to place, bedding down anywhere they could, living off of the land until they found a spot that made them feel welcome. In Richard's case, it seemed anywhere his family tried to build, businesses came in search of land to buy, never paying fair market value, and sometimes not even paying for the land, claiming it as eminent domain.

He had spent his whole life unsettled and desperate for a peaceful existence. Richard wanted a secure life, there could be no peace always being on the move. He dreamed of settling down, becoming closer to his wife, he wanted to be known as a man who believed in God, a man free to worship and have a right to his religion, to serve his Lord the way he wanted, no matter the color of his skin or breed. Too many times this left him on the outskirts of modern religion, especially in these mountains where there was one church house, which also doubled as a primer school house. Life wasn't easy, it never had been and Richard figured it never would be, but he knew it could be better than what he had left behind.

Richard worshipped and prayed at home, atop his mountain as close to God as he had ever been. He may have been ahead of his time, because he was comfortable with everyone else's right to worship the way they saw fit. He never looked down on any man or woman for how they chose to live. Richard believed there was never a winner in a battle of violence, just death or permanent physical and emotional scars. That's why it was so important for him to find the right place to settle, because there had already been too much violence, the Trail of Tears and its history proved that. He often wondered how many graves were along that trail. Too many, and Richard wanted peace more than anything. He always said, "Hatred has no place in the world. We are all here for one reason or another." Strictly speaking, it's a shame more people can't agree about that.

The first summer came and went, it was hot and humid during June and July, even August was sweltering, but the trio forged onward and the log cabin was complete just as the first nip of cold seeped into the mountains, settling in with a bitter chill he would never fully become accustomed to. The cold, brisk wind whipped around upon the hilltop, whistling through the cracks in the log cabin, but when the sun shined brightly they were the first to feel the warmth radiating upon their humble dwelling. Of course the family could now warm themselves near a fireplace, which was much appreciated on damp, frigid nights.

Richard learned what it was to feel true contentment on his mountain top. He discovered that he worried less that someone would come along and run him and his family off. As for Pearl, she smiled and hummed as she tidied their comfortable abode. She kept the small cabin warm and aromatic with the smell of percolated coffee brewing above the fire. She and her sister Dawn had discovered coffee beans, after tasting the deliciously warm liquid at the local commissary, this is also where Dawn met a man she would soon become engaged to, down at the foot of the mountain where David worked at the train depot. He struck up a conversation with Dawn one day, which lead to weekly visits and long discussions. Soon enough, Dawn and David escaped the locals who gathered at the commissary every evening to socialize, the pair went for long walks and picnics until winter's chill made it impossible to take their walks. Winter in the mountains could be brutal. Especially when you lived on top of a hill.

Pearl was pleased that her younger sister had met someone so special. Each night during the coldest months the two women gathered around the warm fire sipping the strong, flavorful hot beverage they both loved, and they spoke of the things that women liked to talk about. Dawn and Pearl enjoyed discussing a spring wedding, as David had already proposed. The women were the most content Richard had ever known them to be. Often times he sat back in his hand- made wicker chair and listened to their excited chatter as they planned the small but important wedding ceremony. Both glowing from excitement. Soon, though, they would discover that Pearl's glow came from other reasons. Just as January snow covered the ground Pearl discovered she was with child. Life couldn't be any better, Richard believed.

Before long, spring was again just around the corner and the ground would thaw from the radiant sun, there was plenty of work ahead as the earth had to be turned over and prepared for their garden. This would be the first real garden for them. Richard had grown a few vegetables in the past, but they had never stayed anywhere long enough to really farm and harvest the land. Richard was happiest when he worked, he was proud to be a strong man, and proud that his wife was going to have their child. He enjoyed their new life and freedom, but he wasn't as comfortable when he went down into the settlement to buy the seeds to plant in his garden. He observed that the people were nice, never overly friendly, they were 'steely eyed', as he had often told Pearl. It seemed the clerks studied him warily, speaking a greeting but nothing more.

Earlier when they had first arrived on the mountain, Richard rarely went down to the settlement, he had much outdoor work, having to make most of his own tools, as it were, thus it was Dawn and Pearl who went to get their necessities. Now that Pearl was with child and Dawn was about to marry, he knew he would have to take on more of the responsibility.

He wished he could be more at ease in the presence of other folk. Richard realized that his trepidation had the potential to make others around him feel even tenser than they normally would. He had noticed two young men in particular who watched him in an odd way, he didn't give much more than a passing thought to it, letting the concern pass on a brief instant of awareness, he was too consumed with getting the items he needed, he had a project he was devoted to and so he didn't watch the two men to see where they went or what they were up to. Richard wanted to make something special for Pearl, she was beaming with a maternal happiness and he wanted to give her a sweet gift. As well, he wanted to make a cradle for their unborn son or daughter. As he picked his items he overheard one young man say to the other, "The little Indian man finally came down off the mountain." But when Richard lifted his eyes to the pair they snickered and turned away. Still, with their backs to Richard, they whispered and pointed.

The mountain boys were a lot taller, younger and heavier than Richard, maybe they didn't have as much physical work to keep them lean, and it was obvious to Richard that they didn't have enough to do to keep them minding their own business, but Richard dismissed their behavior and took his wares home in the wagon he had made for trips to the valley. He felt immediate relief to be back on the mountain top where no one ever bothered them.

Richard not only made the cradle for the baby but he made a rocking chair for Pearl. After Dawn married, he gave her the bed he had made for her when they first built the cabin which opened up just enough space for the sturdy rocking chair and cradle. Pearl was joyfully happy. She patted her husband's hand and gave it a squeeze, "I can't wait until our son or daughter finally arrives."

"It will be the happiest day of our lives." He gave her a kiss on the forehead. He felt it was entirely possible that he had never loved her more.

Spring turned into summer and much work was directed in their garden, Richard and Pearl were a very good team, but Pearl was having a harder time working outside in the merciless heat. Richard carried cool spring water to her and gave her special attention. Late evenings he encouraged her to soak her swollen feet. Richard picked up most of her chores. They missed having Dawn's help, but she was now building her own life with her new husband. The little wedding ceremony had turned out nice, even Richard thought so. He had met several of the people he had only previously saw in passing down at the settlement and learned some of their names. Which made his trips easier when he traveled to the foot of the mountain. A few people even spoke to him and asked about Pearl. By now, Pearl's expanding belly had announced to everyone that a new member of the family was on the way, and most of the ladies asked about Pearl when she could no longer make the trip down into the valley, asking Richard when the baby might be due. This question always brought a jolt of excitement, Richard knew that as the days shortened that the birth of his child would be soon.

Indeed it was early one fall morning when Pearl went into labor. Richard stayed by her side to comfort her, bringing her cool water to dampen her sweat drenched face. He stayed close by her side to be at her beck and call. It seemed to Richard that the labor was long and rough, he had never seen Pearl in so much pain, and her face would become almost purple from strain. As the hours passed he grew more concerned, even though Richard had never attended a human birth he recognized that the labor was taking a toll on his beloved wife. How he wished Dawn was still around to help, but since she had married she had been busy forming her own life, her sister and brother n law mostly neglected.

He pondered walking down to the camp to get a midwife but that would take a while and Richard feared leaving Pearl alone. At one point he kneeled on bended knee and said a prayer, asking that God ease her suffering. It seemed that Pearl was growing so tired, he feared what might happen if birth didn't come soon.

Richard's baby boy was born almost 24 hours after the onset of labor, Pearl was exhausted. However, he could see the joy in her eyes and he felt immense pride and love as he cradled his newborn. Richard had witnessed births of horses and cows and he knew to cut the umbilical cord and tie it off, he knew to clean the baby up and wrap him in a warm blanket where he laid their son in Pearl's arms. Richard did his best at cleaning his wife up as well, he had never had to do this, but she had lost a lot of blood so he burned all of the bloody linens to prevent attracting unwanted animals to their cabin.

He made a soothing tea for Pearl and fed her spoons full of honey, hoping to help rebuild her energy. She and their baby boy were wrapped up in blankets, both asleep when Richard finally took a nap. Hours later he was awakened to the unfamiliar sound of a weak cry from his baby. He saw that Pearl was trying to nurse their son. She looked at Richard, "He must be hungry." She said. But the baby was fussy and didn't seem interested in taking the nipple and Pearl gave her husband a worried look.

Richard moved around to peer over her shoulder at the tiny, infant face, "He seems tired to me. After all, you both had a hard night." Richard told Pearl, "I should make you some broth, as it will help bring your milk in and it will be easy for you to digest. Would you like a bowl of warm bone broth?"

"Yes. I think so." She replied weakly.

Richard warmed the soup for her, wondering how she would eat while holding the baby, after all, he wasn't accustomed to being a father yet, which made him grin, as he was, after all, now a father. "Would you want me to put him in the cradle so you can feed yourself, or….?" Richard was even willing to spoon feed her. All she had to do was ask.

Pearl reached their son out to him. "Would you kindly put him in the cradle?" She asked weakly.

When Richard lifted the sleeping infant from her arms he was aware of how light their son felt. The proud father studied his son's tiny button nose and small lips. He was wrapped so snuggly in the blanket that he hardly stirred when Richard took him from Pearl and placed him gently in the cradle that he had made for their baby.

He turned to his wife who was watching after him curiously, "Get you a good belly full of warm soup, my dear, and then get some more rest. It's best to nap when the baby does. I have to cut some more wood for the fire." Richard told Pearl and made his way outside to do his daily chores.

Richard had always enjoyed a hard day's work in the past, although tiring it was physically rewarding to see a task or chore done to completion. But on this special day, the work was more rewarding than ever. As he busied himself fetching water from the spring, pulling some of the last of the crops from the garden, and chopping wood for the fire, he felt more invigorated than ever. His family was now more complete than it had ever been, he and Pearl were parents. His firstborn was a son, and they needed to give him a proper name. They had discussed naming him after Richard, and it seemed only fitting since he was their first son. They had also discussed naming the baby after her father. Perhaps they could combine the two names. Both Richard and Pearl hoped to have more children, but right now he had a brand new baby boy waiting for him. A son who needed a name. So he carried some wood inside, asking as he entered, "Pearl, have you thought more about what we are going to name our boy?'

He heard Pearl calling out, "Richard, please hurry with that fire!" Her voice was thick and demanding.

Richard saw her sitting on the rocking chair, rocking their baby in her arms as she stared down at the infant. He sat the wood down near the fireplace, "Pearl, I'm getting around to it, but what's the trouble? It's not cold in here."

"The baby is cold." There was something about her voice that alarmed Richard.

He immediately went to his wife and peered down at the baby, recognizing immediately that the infant's face held no color. He reached down and lifted their deceased child from Pearl's arms. Richard's heart sank as he held the baby out and began unwrapping the blanket, looking for any visible reason for the cause of his son's death.

Pearl reached up, tugging at the blanket, "No, Richard! Wrap him back in it, he's cold, Richard."

Richard's gaze went to her tear rimmed eyes, wide with worry and although she was in great denial, he believed Pearl knew but couldn't accept that their baby had died. "I will tend to him." He turned away and dabbed at a single tear as it slid down his cheek, his heart hammering in his chest and his stomach aching as a solid knot ached in pain.

Again Pearl called after him, "Richard, wrap the baby in the blanket." She pleaded.

Richard couldn't believe this was happening. He examined his child and saw nothing that didn't seem right about his perfect little body, except that it was already turning ashen-gray. He wrapped him back in the blanket and carried him to the cradle, aware that Pearl was watching anxiously.

He kneeled beside of the cradle and spoke a silent prayer, turned to Pearl who was now sobbing quietly, "Our baby is dead, Pearl." The pain that washed over her face proved that she hadn't accepted or fully recognized what was happening.

"He got too cold." She stammered. "He was so cold when I got him out of the cradle." And she began to rock in the rocking chair hard, her eyes fixed on the floor, "We shouldn't have laid him in that cold cradle so far away from the fire, so far away from me."

Richard looked at their small, humble home, everything was centered around the fireplace. The fireplace was where they cooked and how they heated the one room cabin. When he built it, he intended to build on to it if their family grew… and that's when Richard felt the full sorrow hit him. He wanted to wilt, to fall down and heave but he knew daylight was slipping away and he had a pine box to build and a hole to dig, "I have to build him a box." He didn't want to leave Pearl, so he prepared her a tea to aid sleeping, suggesting she close her eyes as he helped his wife into bed and gave her a warm cup of tea, covered her in blankets and went outside. It was the hardest thing Richard ever had to build. A small box to bury his son in. He dug a hole deeper than he truly needed to, he did not want any animal to dig his son out of the ground. He finished just before dusk. Tomorrow there would be a funeral. He didn't know how he, or Pearl would hold up when it came time to lay their hours' old infant to rest.

The following days were a blur. A sad, sickening blur. Richard attended the informal burial alone, Pearl refused to leave the house. When he placed the homemade pine box in the ground Richard prayed through his tears. For the first time in his life, he allowed himself to cry fully. He knew Pearl was crying from inside the cabin. She agonized hourly, refusing to believe their baby was dead, and at times blaming him, at other times blaming God. Richard didn't know who to blame.

Days passed with Pearl not speaking to her husband, staring solemnly at the walls. When Richard suggested he visit Dawn to bring her to help, Pearl would cry and shake her head against the suggestion. She had lost her appetite and refused to eat. Richard was torn, he didn't want to leave his wife, yet he knew he needed to find something to help her feel better. He told her softly, "I have to walk down to the camp to get a few things. Do you want me to bring back anything in particular, Pearl?" He hoped against hope that she would say something, but she turned her eyes away from him and shook her head.

Richard returned home hours later, with herbs and food to help soothe pain, aid with sleep and healing, he found Pearl holding an empty blanket in her arms similar to how she had held their baby, rocking and singing to the empty blanket as tears slipped into her dry mouth.

Richard went to her and tried to coax her back

into bed, telling her that she needed to sleep, but when he tried to take the blanket Pearl slapped at him. Her accusing eyes wounding his heart.

As the days multiplied Richard did everything he knew to do, he even returned to the settlement to ask one of the clerks named Hattie for advice, "Pearl won't eat and doesn't even sleep since the baby passed away. I have tried giving her chamomile tea, burdock root tea, and tea with ginger. Nothing helps. She is losing weight. I don't know what to do."

The kind woman looked at Richard, her concern obvious. She knew he was a man of few words. He and his wife had lived around there for nearly two years and she had only seen him a few times. He spoke if he had to, he always nodded a courteous nod of acknowledgement at anyone he met, but rarely did he have much conversation. She looked down at his hands, dropped at his sides, his shoulders slightly slumped, "I am so sorry about the baby. Maybe she needs a female to talk to. I will drop by to visit her, and will bring some home cooked soup up to your house this evening, we must get her to eat something hearty."

Richard said, "I have made potato soup, vegetable soup and even carried fresh greens for salads to her, those were her favorites and she has refused them all."

The woman paused in consideration, "Let me try, Richard, maybe she would be able to talk to me, and release her sorrows. She might fancy a pot of pinto beans and cornbread." Hattie suggested, "I will be sure to bring enough to last a few days."

This wasn't the help Richard was searching for, but he gave her a nod of gratitude and turned away. Just as he reached the door to exit the woman asked of him, "What happened to the baby? Was it stillborn?"

Richard stopped walking and stiffened his spine, the pain flooding his soul. "I reckon so." Was all he could say, he didn't have any answers, but it was no one's business if his child was born dead or alive, the fact remained the little infant had only lived hours and his wife was grieving herself to death and Richard had no idea what to do. He strode out of the building to return home. Knowing that the pinto beans wouldn't entice Pearl to eat. He hoped a visit from Hattie would give Pearl hope. Instead, when Hattie and two of her friends came, Pearl listened and gave a weak nod for their kindness, but she didn't seem interested in their company.

Out of desperation Richard made his way to his sister n law's home. Dawn had only visited a few times since she had married, and when he saw her he immediately wished he hadn't made the trip. Her small swell of a belly confirmed that she too was expecting a little one. Richard explained to Dawn that he had hoped her visit might lift Pearl's spirits, but he worried that when Pearl saw that Dawn was expecting a baby that her depression might deepen. Dawn felt immediate guilt, "I should have come around more." She cried, "I had no idea how bad things were for you and Pearl. I was so consumed with my own life." She sobbed heavily into the palms of her hands. Richard wished he had the words to comfort her but he didn't even have the correct words to comfort his wife. He told Dawn to use her own judgement in regards to visiting Pearl.

A few evenings later Dawn and her husband David brought Pearl a basket of fresh vegetables. Dawn wore a loose dress, but the roundness of her stomach occasionally showed. Whether Pearl noticed or not was beyond any of their knowledge as she hardly spoke to anyone. In fact it seemed that the visit brought additional sadness as she wiped away at the tears which brimmed her eyes when Dawn placed the basket at Pearl's feet before bending over for a hug. Richard hoped no one would mention the baby, and no one did. Perhaps avoiding the topic did more harm than good. But who could have known?

Within two weeks Richard found himself digging yet another grave atop his hillside right next to their son, where Pearl was laid to rest. Richard found 2 heavy stones and chiseled the dates of their deaths into each stone. He also built a picket fence around the graves, leaving just enough room beside Pearl for one more grave, though who would dig his grave when the time arrived, he didn't even ponder.

Even though Richard's pain was deep and he felt lonesome, he busied himself as best he could. The next time the women from the camp came to check on Pearl, he had to tell them with a heavy heart that she had passed away.

Little did he know at the time Hattie and her women friends would carry the news to the encampment and from there word would travel, with unanswered questions about Richard's silence and reluctance to come down into the settlement. Horrid speculations that the baby and Pearl had died of unnatural causes also circulated. After all, no one had ever seen the baby, they had seen Pearl definitely swollen with child, but they had never actually seen the baby. When the women had visited Pearl, carrying her food and vegetable plates she had looked weak and malnourished, and older. She had aged ten years. She hadn't spoken to anyone, her dark eyes following their every move but her lips never parted to make a sound. Richard had no way of knowing these things were being said because he had no desire to leave his cabin or the land surrounding it. He would have been especially hurt had he known that Dawn herself had questioned why he had kept the baby's birth and death a secret, and why had he not called for her sooner, seeking help.

Until one day before the cold months reached the mountain he decided he needed to go to the commissary to buy some dry goods, to help him when he wouldn't be able to get outside to work during snows and wet weather. Richard greeted those who spoke, gave a courteous nod to those who watched his every move. He sensed that their demeanor had changed, they seemed overly watchful.

"Well there's that little Indian hermit." He heard a male voice say from behind him. He turned and saw the same two young men who had made a similar comment in the past. One said to the other, "It's about time he came down off his mountain top. Guess he has something to hide up there. Must be the reason he don't want no visitors or don't come around anybody and be friendly." The other one laughed and started to make a wise crack but Richard turned to face them squarely and he told them, "My business is none of your business."

His reply caught them by surprise, perhaps they didn't expect such a quiet man to have a voice. However, his words weren't a deterrent.

That's when one said, "It might not be nobody's business unless something fishy is going on, like why you had to go and bury your wife and baby, what happened to them, little hermit?"

There was an awkward silence, everyone within hearing distance stood completely still. Richard didn't blink, he didn't waver, and he didn't want to be enticed into an argument, so he thought for a moment, swallowing his anger before speaking, "Every man's got to take care of his own, and I intend to take care of whatever is mine. Right now, I am taking care not to get angry about the nonsense spewing from your mouths. You don't know anything about which you speak." He paused, looked at both of the young men and the people nearby as he went on to say, "And my name is not *the little hermit*. You will address me by Mr. Thorpe." He didn't stand around to hear their comeback, he went to the clerk and paid her for his goods and left.

Never displaying the range of emotions which had surged through his tense body.

However, the silent accusations implied by their words never left him, nor were far from his thoughts. How could anyone believe he would deliberately harm his wife and newborn infant? Many nights went by as he slept restlessly, awaking to bad dreams and dark thoughts. Until the darkness of his heart and mind swallowed him whole, and he went about his days doing chores and that which had to be done, with no conscious effort or awareness. Waiting for the night to engulf him then he slept the restless sleep of a man in deep mourning.

After one of the longest winters of his life, Richard began to feel the darkness lifting and the coldness thawing inside himself. He began to explore the perimeters of the land, searching for what he didn't know, just searching. He was trying to keep his mind from the darkness and sadness which had consumed him. He realized he needed more than just his cabin and his garden. He hoped an idea or discovery would spawn from his exploration, it seemed that his God always provided if he was patient enough to wait it out. One day when he was walking the land, swiping aside small trees in his path, he heard a soft whimpering nearby, an animalistic whimper which was weak and carried the hint of fear on the tail end of the whimper. He followed the sound until he found a small opening in the side of the earth with some rocks and dirt that had slid down around the opening, which wasn't large to begin with. As he approached the den the sounds of whimpering silenced. He studied the hole curiously, cautiously. He had no idea what was trapped in the hole, it could be a wild animal. After a few minutes the whimper started back, a little softer, more cautious than before. Perhaps it was a baby wild animal and the mother was away, but Richard wanted to know what was whining in the hole. He kneeled down and looked into the darkness, seeing nothing, but he smelled the familiar scent of a dog. He knew from experience that wild animals had a more pungent and musky odor. This scent seemed to be more domestic. Richard gave a soft call to the animal which paused in silence, then panted, then whined again.

He began pulling the rocks and dirt away from the hole with both hands, the frightened animal inside became silent until Richard had opened a large enough hole for the dog to stick its muzzle out for fresh air. Richard pulled at the rocks faster. Finally the dog emerged. Its fur was so dirty it was difficult to tell what color its coat was. As it stepped forward Richard saw how sickly looking and rail thin it was. Richard allowed the animal to sniff his hand, which it did reluctantly. When it finally gave his knuckles a thankful lick Richard scooped the dog up into his arms and carried it home.

That's how Lucky came into his life. He nursed the animal back to health, it was a medium sized, mixed variety, and Richard was thankful to have its companionship. The dog ate with Richard, slept at the foot of the bed and watched after the cabin. Lucky followed him everywhere he went, even when he gardened. One day he and Lucky went back to the den where he originally found the dog. It turned out the hole Lucky had been trapped in seemed to be an opening to a small cavern.

Finding the dog and the cave was a blessing to Richard, it kept his mind off of the loss of his family, and although he sank more and more into a solitary lifestyle, Richard forged on, visiting the mouth of the cave daily if weather permitted, as he carefully constructed a brace for the entrance which he dug out slowly and cautiously with a pick and shovel. On hot days it was cool inside of the little cavern, and Richard constructed a small bench, where he and Lucky bided the hottest part of mid-day at the mouth of what he fancied as his very own cave. Richard often enjoyed how his voice sounded as he sang at the opening of the cavern. Sometimes Lucky added to the song with a lonesome howl, other days he slept at his owner's feet. When the dog bored of passing time this way, Lucky chose a stone or a stick to gnaw on, always near his master.

Both the man and his dog were equally adept at observing, learning to use what nature provided and surviving with little more than what they yielded atop their hill. In fact, it was Lucky who carried the first piece of coal from the small cavern, munching on it with more than a passive interest. Richard was happy to discover that now he could gather coal and wood from his land, and cavern, to help him with building his fire for cooking and in the winter months to heat the small cabin. Although he had lost more than he would ever be able to replace when he lost his wife and son, the good Lord had given him everything he needed. In his deepest thoughts he wished Pearl and their son were here to enjoy it alongside him.

He rarely went down into the settlement, except for when he needed dry goods such as flour, meal, sugar and coffee. He and Lucky would walk into the camp with a wooden wagon pulled behind "the Hermit", as the people called him, and he bought what he needed no more often than once every other month. Richard was scarcely aware of how fascinated the locals were with his life until one day Lucky stood up from his noon time nap and started barking at something Richard couldn't quite yet see.

He stood up from his rocking chair, the same one Pearl had rocked their infant in, and watched down the path as four men appeared, walking in an irregular line, with one man dressed fancier than the others, he wore what Richard would assume a business man might wear. Two of the other men carried boxes, one with a handle on it, Richard guessed this black box was a case carried by business men. The other large, odd shaped box was a device he had never seen before, nor recognized.

When the men approached, a well-groomed, well-dressed man pushed around in front of the others to extend a hand of greeting, "Richard Thorpe?" When Richard gave a firm pump of the hand and a nod of the head the man continued, "I am Bert Vincent, with The Knoxville News Sentinel newspaper."

Richard had never been to Knoxville, but had heard about it, "Aren't you a little far away from home?" He inquired as his dark brown eyes scanned all of the men standing around. He recognized two of them as locals whom he had never even had a conversation with.

"I write a column about life here in the Appalachian mountains, my column is known as 'Strolling with Bert'. Recently someone wrote a letter to the editor of the newspaper about a Cherokee Indian man who lived all alone up here on the land he found and laid claim to, the land he turned into his homestead." Bert paused and studied Richard carefully who was in return, studying him just as warily, "They call you the little Indian Hermit. Don't be offended." Bert said with haste and a chuckle, as he sensed Richard's discomfort, "The people who live down at the foot of the mountain are astonished at how you live here on this hilltop surviving on your own, making almost everything yourself." He didn't pause for very long, "They know that you make your own medicines and tools and everything from scratch. And they know how hot it gets up here in the summer, even more than that, how bitterly cold you probably get in the harsh winter months. When they see a foot of snow you probably have two or three times that much snow up here." Bert kept waving his hand across the skyscape, as Richard really was as close to the top of the mountain as anyone could be.

"I stopped at the country store to ask how to find you, and these men said they would have to show me how to get up here. It's not easy to navigate or find you, Mr. Thorpe, I never would have been able to find you on my own, especially not at the gap of the mountain, not without their help."

Richard had never read the newspaper, he barely was able to read at all. As far as he knew Mr. Vincent had no reason to lie about who he was, "What made you look for me? Don't most people live as I live?" He knew that in these parts most people had a garden, many had built their own house or the family helped build it with them. Land was handed down to generations, maybe this generation hadn't acquired their land the same way he had, but somehow the first family had to acquire theirs in a similar fashion.

"Not exactly, Mr. Thorpe." Bert chuckled, amazed at how humble and unimpressed this fella was. "You did all of this," and again Bert waved his arm across the span of the land which included the simple log cabin, the furniture, the wagons and carts that he had made, a massive garden, massive for one man, but he grew such a variety of things. "You did this ALL by yourself."

Richard tensed for a moment, "Well, I had Pearl help me at first."

Bert had already learned from some of the people in the country store about Pearl, his wife, and about the baby. He had asked some questions and had heard that some people thought maybe Pearl herself had killed the baby is the reason she went stark raving mad, and died from a shameful guilt. Others speculated that Richard had tried to doctor her himself and actually caused her death. Or maybe he had caused the baby's death. No one knew for sure if the baby was born alive. Even Pearl's sister had no idea. Dawn had only learned of the birth and subsequent death after the infant had been buried. At this point she had never ventured back to Richard's home after the last visit to see her grieving sister, when she saw with her own eyes that Pearl was mentally ill. She had heard of her sister's death weeks later along with the viscous rumors and Dawn had worried if there was any truth to them. Bert had already stopped by her home and interviewed Dawn before being escorted to Richard's home.

In fact, after interviewing Dawn, Bert was even more interested in the Cherokee Indian man. She had verified how Richard was a practicing medicine man back when they had lived in Cherokee. In fact, in those days he had sold his elixirs with promises of cure and wealth. He had sold herbs, handmade salves and ointments all along the trails as they journeyed forward, Richard sold whatever he *could* sell, until the day they discovered this mountain top where he now dwelled. However, a medicine man was in no way a practicing doctor. Medicine men worked with natural herbs and created potions and elixirs. Most of their medicines were steeped in pure superstition. Dawn and the people at the camp wondered if Richard had tried a potion on Pearl that might have hastened her demise.

"Pearl was your wife?" Bert asked softly. "She is buried up here somewhere, isn't she? Along with your infant son?"

Richard gave a slight nod. "You didn't travel all this far just to stand here and ask that. What do you really want?"

Bert was surprised but not shocked by the man's reaction and he knew if he didn't tread carefully he would lose the chance at writing the article. "I would like to interview you and write about your life here in the mountains. I will do your story justice. People from outside these mountains are fascinated with such stories. I have several of my columns in the newspapers here with me for you to look at if you want to see my writings."

That's when one of the men lifted up the carrying case and opened the box for Richard to see a small stack of newspapers. Richard didn't need to read anything, he would never see the Knoxville News Sentinel, but he accepted the papers one man handed to him and he looked at Bert hard, "This won't lead to any sort of nonsense, will it?" He asked.

"Nonsense? What do you mean?" Bert inquired.

"I won't have to worry about any tax revenuer's or business men coming around to take my land or demand money from me, will I?"

Bert gave a light hearted chuckle, "This article will not give directions to your home, I would never be able to find my way back without these men, so believe me, and I don't think anyone will come after you to take your land."

And so Richard spoke to Bert Vincent, answering his questions and he soon learned that the odd shaped box being carried by one of the men was a camera and that his photograph would appear in the newspaper. Richard didn't exactly like the idea, but he was happy when the interview concluded, waving a sign of farewell as the men departed. Hoping the column was interesting and brought Mr. Vincent more readers, but wondering how it could interest others because he lived such a simple life.

That evening he and Lucky sat around the old fire, he played his guitar and sang his favorite song, *"Over the Hill to the Poor House."*, when he reached the chorus Lucky always howled with him, it said, *"I'm old, I'm helpless and feeble, And the days of my youth have gone by, And over the hills to the poor house, I must wander alone there to die."*
He knew he would become a lonely, aged, old man. Richard held no hope that he would ever remarry. How could he when he never went anywhere to meet someone? It didn't worry him much, because he would never be able to bear the pain of losing someone he loved again, his heart had been so broken by the loss of his beloved wife and only son.

31

It must have been about six weeks after that day when the first of the curiosity seekers came up the path. Once again Lucky sounded out a rapid onslaught of barks, quietened only when his master stood next to him. Richard saw two women and one man approaching rather sheepishly. One of the women spoke first, "Richard Thorpe?" She knew it was him from the photograph printed with the article, "We read the column in the news sentinel about you." She still appeared hesitant to get on with what she wanted to say.

Richard stiffened considerably. He hadn't thought about that column since the day Bert Vincent came onto his property.

The lady continued, "I was wondering, if you might have some of that elixir on hand that you used to make. The one to cure stomach ailments." She pointed to the man beside her, "My husband here, he has bad stomach pain and at times he doubles over and he can't even go to work because of it."

Richard was surprised. He had mentioned to the reporter that he had stopped making the medicines that Dawn had told the columnist about. Richard answered with firmness, "I don't make nothing for sale to others, and I only make what I need… or what a family member might need." He paused as he thought about his situation, and the medicines he had made in effort to save Pearl, and her mother before her. "I don't have any family anymore, so I don't have any elixirs to give or sell, nor will I make any more."

The women exchanged confused looks, as if they had been told one story and Richard was telling another. "You're not an herb doctor?' And quickly the second woman asked, "You don't make love potions, neither?" She had read in the article that he used to sell love potions and tonics roadside before settling in Tennessee.

"I never claimed I was any such thing!" He retorted.

"But the paper said you made tonics and potions!" One lady exclaimed.

Richard sucked in his breath, "I knew that pesky newspaper would bring trouble! I don't sell medicine or potions anymore!!!! Now if you will kindly leave me be. If you can spread the word that I want to be left alone up here, *and* if any other writer wants to ask questions about me, you can spread the word that I am not interested in talking to anyone!"

It seemed his request fell on deaf ears, a few days later different people approached him, snooping around as if looking for things that they could steal. Richard didn't have much. He stopped one man and asked him, "What in tarnation are you looking for?" He caught the man near the graves he had made for his wife and infant son.

The man stammered and fumbled and finally said, "They are saying all sorts of things about you, old man!!! Don't you know? They talk about how you have jars of money hidden up here and how you are mining something out of a cave!!"

Richard suddenly was overcome with anger, as he realized someone had been spying on him. He began screaming and hollering and ordering the man off his property, "If I ever catch you on my land again I will send you back down that path with buckshot in the seat of your pants!!"

That evening he made a few wooden signs, etching the words "Keep out!" on the boards and he stuck them in various places around his property. Richard had barely learned to read or write, but thankfully he knew those words, he wished he could have written more, as in, "Trespassers will be shot!" but he definitely didn't know how to spell trespassers.

One morning he discovered that someone had taken his wooden signs, had removed the rocks that marked Pearl's grave along with the rock that marked the baby's grave and had even kicked down the wooden fence he had built around the small graves.

Richard was determined to put an end to this nonsense, to set the record straight. That evening as he and his dog strolled into town, he noticed that every person in plain sight stopped what they were doing and watched him. He decided that he needed to get the point across, so he went to the local market and he spoke as loud as he could to the bystanders, "A bunch of your people have been coming upon my land, snooping around, talking nonsense and bothering me. Today I find out that some person came up overnight and tore down the fence I made and pulled up markers on the graves of my wife and baby. Let this be a warning to you and anyone who is thinking about coming up there to bother me…" He paused and looked and saw that the two young men who often watched him and made snide remarks were more than interested in his little demonstration. Richard squared his shoulders and said, "I will let my old shotgun do the talking to the next people who comes around and tries to take or damage anything I own."

He took a long look at every face turned in his direction. He saw that one lady dropped her face but then she looked at him evenly, and her mouth opened but then she closed it and tried to turn away.

Richard knew she had something important to say, "Ma'am, you there," he pointed and she turned towards him with cheeks blushing, "Did you have something you meant to tell me?"

She nodded and looked around at the onlookers, "As a matter of fact, I believe I do know why this is happening to you." She approached him closer, so she could lower her voice, "People around here have been talking about you for a long time now, they think you are….peculiar." She spat the word out as if it tasted bad. "That's why that city man came up here to write a story about you. Before that people thought you or your wife were crazy plain and simple. But then that story made it appear as if you could make potions and cures and that you were getting gold or silver or something out of a mine you found… and also, there's a lot of these people think you got paid a lot of money for the story. And well, people say you buried jars of money up there on that hill, next to the graves." She paused, then added, "Where DO you get your money, since you have no job?'

Richard couldn't believe what he was hearing. He was glad he had traveled down into the settlement now, "I can promise you there is no gold or silver up there anywhere, and there are no jars of money, I didn't get paid a single cent for that story." He spoke loud enough for all to hear as every person within hearing range still watched him, wearily and sheepishly. "Where I get my money is my business. Now I want you to spread the message I just spoke instead of spreading all this gossip." He stated and turned to walk away.

That's when the two men who had given him trouble in the past spoke up, "Well aren't you just the feisty little runt. Always coming around acting high and mighty but never doing a friendly thing for anyone." The tallest said. Then his friend chimed in, "I reckon you think you can move right into this camp and live on the outskirts and do everything your way. And that we all have to abide by *your* rules. Is that what you are thinking?'"

Richard looked at them hard in the eyes, his jaws clamped tight enough to cause the muscles to clinch, then he relaxed his posture, assumed a submissive curtsy and turned away from the two men who were trying to antagonize him. He walked quietly away, but he heard the snickers and the whispers, even though he couldn't make out the words. He felt all of their eyes as they bore into his back, and he hoped none of them decided to follow him. He had said all he wanted to say, there was nothing more to discuss.

Days passed with Richard on high alert, but as weeks passed he felt the tension easing and he began to go about his daily chores just as he had always done. Then one evening at dusk as he and Lucky took a break at the mouth of the cave, he heard footsteps and voices spoken in low tones, his dog heard it, too and began to bark. Richard touched the dog's back and petted him into silence. He hoped the intruders would leave, because he wasn't close to his house and his rifle was in the cabin. He didn't want to shoot anyone but he had planned on shooting into the air as a warning sign the next time anyone bothered him.

Richard kept his hands on Lucky's head, holding him by the scruff of his neck, pulling him close, and then he pulled the dog into the cave with him as he heard footsteps getting closer. He hoped the dog would remain silent. The animal seemed to sense his caution and the dog and the man remained still as they heard voices.

A male voice could be heard saying, "He's been seen digging right around here. That old man's been digging in this cavern for a while now, he ain't diggin' for no reason."

A different voice said, "If he's found gold or silver or anything like that, we're taking it all. He might even have a moonshine steel or something hid in there. It's about time we run this old man off from here."

The other man snorted, "He can't take on the two of us. We will surprise him. He's broken down and getting old..." the voices stopped.

Richard knew they were just seconds away from finding him, and he bent slowly to pick up the pick-axe he used to dig for coal. He didn't want it to be this way, but he knew what was about to happen.

One of the men said, "Look." And the footsteps stopped just outside the cavern. Richard realized they had discovered the mouth of the cavern.

Lucky looked up at his master and the Cherokee Indian man looked deep into the dog's eyes. It was as if they communicated silently because just as the two men started walking towards the opening of the cavern Richard let out a war cry that would curdle the blood in anyone's veins and Lucky let out a growl and the two sprang into action. Richard moved swiftly and with the strength of a much bigger man, he brought one of the men down, using the handle of the axe, not the sharp blade, while Lucky jumped the other fella and the two men found themselves on the ground, kicking at the hermit man and his dog. Richard grabbed one of the men by the hair on his scalp and drug him along the ground, his Cherokee war cry ringing in his ears and with one blow to the head knocked the man out cold. The other man was trying to punch at the dog who had a hold on his arm, teeth sinking into flesh. He saw the hermit man approaching with something in his hand held up high above his head and then he saw blackness.

If it wasn't for the fact another man saw it all happen, the story might never had been passed down. But this man was supposed to be their look out, when he heard the commotion he hunkered down behind trees and watched as one Cherokee Indian man and his dog drug the two unconscious men down to the well house and watched as the old man hoisted up a bucket of water, he poured the water over the two men's head. When the men came to, Richard stood with axe in hand, holding it over them as if he might chop the axe blade into their skulls. They scampered to get up and Richard kicked both of their feet out from under them. "I chose to let you live this time. There better not be a next time." Then he kicked dirt upon them and raised the axe even higher, "Now git!!!!"

The two men stood up and ran, it was the same two men who had mouthed off to Richard in the past. The third man waited until Richard went inside his cabin before he went back down the hill. There was no way he wanted to get caught by the Indian hermit man.

From that day forward when Richard came into the camp people were courteous, although stand-offish, most barely spoke because they knew the quiet man could fly off the handle and tales circulated about his eccentric ways, but more than that, tales circulated how a small framed, Cherokee Indian man took on two big country boys and "whooped them both single handed, knocking them out cold!"

Tales carry, they always do, truth mingled with fiction until it's hard to separate the two, but much of this story is based on truth, and the tale has lived on, long after Richard was gone from his mountain top. You see I know, because Richard Thorpe was my great, great Uncle. In the end, the quiet little man earned a community's respect and after his demise people dug around on his land for years after he died, searching for his money, or gold or silver buried in jars. Or any relic they could carry off which once belonged to "the little hermit".

The end

Ben

By T.R. Love & J. Poore

This is a story of courage and possibly love between two people down on their luck, who just happen to be of different races. This is the story of Ben and Red. Their story begins decades ago. We have all been told that history repeats itself and if you live long enough, chances are you will see that it's true. It seems in this present day, history is repeating.

As the red haired, tall lady stood at the casket, she held the hand of her daughter. Her skin was clammy and she was on the verge of tears. She looked down into the casket at the African-American man lying there, in his best suit and tie, giving all appearances he was simply asleep.

The red haired woman was numb, she had just learned of his passing the day before. As she looked at him, every line on his face as familiar as her own, she felt her heart skip a beat, and she clung tighter to her daughter's hand. "Oh, Ben." She whispered as a single tear slipped into the corner of her mouth. Her mind awhirl with unanswered questions.

Sadly Ben's life had been cut short, and both women inwardly wondered how it could have possibly happened. If he had lived through the turbulent and violent times of prejudice and hatred, then what could have brought this strong man down? He had earned his place as a respected black man in a white man's world. The red haired woman knew this all too well, since she had walked through several chapters of life with him.

As Red looked upon the body of Ben in the casket with a tear in her eye she silently asked him, 'How? They didn't kill either one of us then, so how did this happen?' The dead man, of course, couldn't answer.

Standing there at the funeral parlor decades after they had met, it took Red back to an era of great prejudice and injustice. It seemed the present was filled with as much anger and resentment as ever before, and in retrospect not much was different from the volatile 1960's and 1970's. When Ben, a solid man of color would meet one of his closest friends, a white woman known as "Red". This is how it all began.

Her real name was Flo and she was a tall, slim woman, who had worked mostly as a waitress, but she had held many jobs over the course of her life. Red had married young at the tender age of 15, by the age of 16 she was already a mother. Barely an adult herself, she had taken on motherhood and adulthood simultaneously, forced into a marriage that neither she nor her husband wanted. Red wasn't liked or appreciated at home, there she was scolded by her husband and reminded daily of their misery which he blamed her for. But at work Red was well liked and admired by her employers and patrons. She was personable and had a sense of humor. Red treated everyone the same. It didn't matter if they were rich or poor, a doctor or a homeless person, and it definitely didn't matter if their skin was a different color from hers.

Ben, on the other hand, had never married nor fathered children of his own, but he had certainly faced many challenges that differed from Red's. He had faced much resistance as he made his way through those challenges. He had grown up the eldest of three sons born to a hard working African-American woman. Theirs had been a life of constant upheaval and Ben had never stayed in any one place for very long.

Ben didn't have a birth-father to guide him, his biological father had left the family before Ben turned 2 years old.

Ben had never even known him. A few years later his mother had married a man who fathered the next 2 boys, and it was this man who had taught Ben and his brothers what it meant to be an upstanding person, to work hard and that nobody was too good to do whatever was necessary to survive, you get what you work for.

Unfortunately, his step-father had been murdered in cold blood on a darkened dead end street late one night in southern Alabama. He wasn't doing anything wrong, at that time he had been working two jobs to help support his family, and he happened to be returning home from work when he got a flat tire. The people who pretended to stop to help actually stopped to rob him and shot him to keep their identities safe. Whoever shot him got away with murder, and the local authorities and media questioned only one thing, why was a black man traveling that late at night in a white neighborhood? Coincidentally, there had been a rash of vehicles broken into, and homes were also broken into over the months prior to the murder and the news media printed the speculation that perhaps this black man was the thief. Ben and his family knew better, but during those days black families didn't have much of a voice. And so his mother moved away from Alabama with her three sons, hoping to form a better life elsewhere. It would be decades later when Ben's path would cross Red's, but both of their past lives would have already prepared them for the battles they would face.

Red was a mother of four children and still unhappily married to the same man when she met and befriended the man named Benjamin, or "Ben" as he was known. She met him at a popular diner where she worked, nestled in the valley of East Tennessee. In those days, down South, white people often referred to a black person as a "colored" person, but the worst among them referred to anyone of color using the unflattering word form of "Negro", but Red wouldn't call a black person the "n" word, and she bristled every time she heard its usage. She knew how much her black friends detested the word being used to degrade them and their race.

As she got to know Ben, along with his friends and family she learned about the injustices present in their lives, and the trials they faced for no other reason than the color of their skin. She learned that sometimes it shamed her the way her fellow white people acted and she was often ashamed of her own white ancestors, some of her friends and even some of her very own family members who made cutting remarks or threatened violent acts against people of color.

Red was a young woman during the civil rights movement and she witnessed many changes, she saw the hatred concealed within most people as it emerged in a swift and frightening manner when change began to take place, but she also saw that some changes were for the improvement of mankind. But too many times, the improvement of humanity came at a bloody cost. Peaceful demonstrations often turned violent and ended in tragedy, although some demonstrations resulted in the change they were intended for, but frequently it caused constant strife between races. Protests and' sit-ins' were happening when Red was working at the greasy spoon diner in a well-known, but small town located in the foothills of East Tennessee.

This was shortly after the assassination of Dr. Martin Luther King JR., the civil rights leader who had started out on a spiritual and peaceful journey to end segregation and civil injustice, but tragic riots, bombings and eventually murder thwarted most of his efforts. Men were divided, white among black, and white against whites. If you spoke openly about wanting to end segregation you risked being beaten. There was so much hardship and sorrow. People lived in a constant state of worry and suffered much grief during these times. Black people weren't allowed to use the public restrooms, or ride in the front seats of public buses or eat in restaurants with the white people, and this went on for far too long even after Dr. King's murder.

Red could remember it happening and it brought shame to her recalling how dreadful some white people treated the black people. This carried on well into the 1970's when Red was working at a little diner during those times, the employees were instructed to feed the blacks at the back door of the restaurant. It didn't make a difference if it was the hottest part of summer or the coldest part of winter, they had to stand outside to eat. This made Red feel very uncomfortable, treating people this way, and so Red spoke softly and kindly to the black families, hoping her kindness softened the blow of being treated so callously.

Eventually demonstrations began in her town, the sit-ins were spreading across the south as more and more black patrons demanded equality, sitting at the counters elbow to elbow with whites, many of whom didn't want to be in the presence of the ethnic group. Red had always told her children, "When the sit-ins started, we didn't know what to expect, we had heard on the news how sometimes people started harassing the colored people, even throwing food at them trying to get them to leave. We didn't know how we were going to handle our new customers, but we were instructed to smile and look happy and to wait on our black patrons as fast as possible so they would leave."

But the purpose behind a "sit-in" was to stay as long as they wanted, as long as they would buy a soda or a cup of coffee, the black patrons could sit in the restaurant. And so Red found herself joking and cutting up even more than usual, perhaps trying to keep peace as she could feel the tension looming thickly in the air as the white folk watched the black folk from the corners of their eyes, many of them making snide remarks under their breath. Red joked and sang to the black patrons, topping off their coffee, teas and soft drinks with a warm, genuine smile, and a song in her heart. This was no different than how she treated the white patrons, the only difference is that her white customers took particular notice that she also treated the black customers this way.

Red had worn a nickname her entire life, because of her red hair, as a result she often gave nicknames to her favorite and regular patrons. All local diners have "regulars", patrons who come in on a consistent basis, often times ordering the same foods, and they are on a first name basis with the waitresses and waiters. Red became familiar with a group of "regulars" who happened to also be a group of black men who had moved to the little town, each searching for a better life.

The three men often came as a group, dropping in several times each week. One of the men Red had nicknamed *Moses*, for his neatly trimmed white beard and kind eyes. The other was a big, tall man who always had a joke or riddle to share and she had given him the nickname *Problem Child*. But then there was Ben, whom Red had never given a nickname to, there was something special about Ben, the way he seemed comfortable anywhere he was, how he silently exhibited self-confidence within himself. Each of these men were well mannered and well dressed, never a moment's trouble. During those days she and Ben and his friends were just casual acquaintances. But soon life tossed them together as their paths often crossed, collided and even entwined and soon it would become them against a small town and its dirty little secrets steeped with racism.

Ben had come from Louisiana, from down in the Bayous. He had worked for a white man named Latemar, who was a judge, perhaps a corrupt judge from the sounds of the story. Red had always been intrigued by Ben's stories, but while serving him at the diner she never could ask many questions, mostly she just caught bits and pieces of his tales, even though he shared some of the stories with her on slower days, but so many questions went unanswered. Such as, why had the Judge told him, "Ben, if you can keep yourself out the graveyard, I will keep you out of jail?" Red never asked Ben what he was doing for the powerful judge. Was it something illegal? That is certainly not anything she dared ask him in a public place during those crucial times, there were too many eyes and ears anxiously awaiting any reason to crucify a black man.

It was only after she and Ben got closer that Red saw the physical scars herself, she could see and feel the rigid stripes across his back where two men had whipped him so hard with leather belts that the fabric of his shirt was embedded in his open gashes, they had whipped him for purely no other reason than he was black. When Red later met Ben's mother, the elderly woman confirmed that she had picked the fabric out of the wounds on her son's back with tweezers. Red often rubbed his back just to feel the scars, it was like rubbing an old washboard.

Ben also had a long, raised scar from under his left ribcage, across his chest to under his right arm from a knife wound. Another incident which resulted from the "job" he did for the judge. He had also been shot in the back with buckshot which left light, pitted scars where some of the pellets stayed in his skin.

One of her favorite stories was how Ben had survived being beaten by a group of white men who tried to hang him and leave him for dead. Luckily Ben was stout and flexible, plus the men didn't know how to hang a person properly because Ben was able to get the rope loosened enough around one wrist to reach into his back pocket for a pocket knife, Ben had told her, "I was desperate to get free, I can't tell you how I wriggled and twisted around , but when I got that blade to my mouth, I used my free hand and mouth to open the blade and cut through the rope, I managed to cut my own tongue in two." Again, he had the scar to prove it, his tongue had a slit in the side of it. Ben had told these stories at the diner to his friends and to Red, and she had enjoyed hearing them, never had she heard about this kind of lifestyle before. Red hadn't known much about the world outside of her own life.

Red's life had mostly been a struggle to keep her family in a warm bed and fed, and yes it had been difficult on her meager wages and tips. As had become the habit of her married life, she and her husband Ralph had moved so many times, out-running the landlords, because one thing Ralph detested was working for a living, he would rather fiddle with broken down junk cars than show up for work regularly. He even resorted to stealing their children's lunch money from his wife's purse when he needed money, which often left them short on rent and other necessities.

So while Ben had been outrunning the law in the Bayous and swamps of Louisiana for a judge named Latemar, Red had been outrunning the debtors, and it wasn't because she wanted to live this way or cheat anyone. Far from it, Red had no choice. Ralph was so unhappy in their marriage that he not only refused to contribute to their livelihood, reminding her often, "If it weren't for you and these children I could have anything I wanted." It seemed Ralph didn't want to accept the fact that he had impregnated Red while she was underage, it seemed he didn't want to admit that he taken advantage of her father and mother while they helped him find a job and allowed him to stay in their home when he was 18 years of age, jobless and homeless, that's how he and Red had met anyway. It seemed he didn't want to accept that he didn't have to marry Red, sure he could have run away from his responsibility and left Red and his child behind, but he went along with her parents and Red to the justice of the peace. He willingly accepted their monetary donation when her parents boarded the pair on a bus that left West Virginia and headed to East Tennessee. Ralph also didn't mind having a wife to screw as much as he wanted, literally and figuratively, but as long as he had her to blame he stayed in the marriage, complaining and harassing her almost daily.

Ben had left Louisiana to be free from the dangerous lifestyle he was living, and to get away from the things he wanted to let go of, he wanted a fresh beginning. Red had felt trapped in her life, she didn't think she had anywhere to go. When she befriended Ben he was a determined man in his thirties, he had grown accustomed to living his life embattled. Judge Latemar had earned the reputation of one person not to cross and his repute wasn't challenged by many, Ben was known as one of *his* men, and this afforded Ben a certain level of protection from his lawless behavior, which even included gambling. It was one of his favored pass times, but like all good things which must come to an end, Ben's luck was starting to run out back in the Bayou's, as more up and rising lawbreakers emerged, challenging Judge Latimar's power, putting Ben at an even greater risk. Ben was growing tired of the worry and having to constantly look over his shoulder. He had made friends with the two men named Alvin (Moses) and Jerard (Problem Child) so when they mentioned that they were leaving for the calmer hills of East Tennessee he decided to pack up and go with them. It seemed a calmer life was calling his name. At least, that was what his intentions had been.

Red was seeking the same thing, a calmer more peaceful life with the ability to pay her bills and keep her family fed, she had saved money for years, hiding as much of her tip money as she could save without putting her family in more of a financial hardship than they already faced. She was saving for a divorce. She wanted to leave Ralph. Had planned on leaving Ralph for years. It was during this time that she and Ben were becoming closer. They were simply friends, both down on their luck, both wanting and needing a better life.

Already they were facing accusations from the people at the diner, who noticed how Red sometimes lingered a little too long at Ben's table. Always cutting up with him and his friends. The supervisor even pulled Red aside one night to question her, "What is going on with you and those colored men?"

Red cringed at the accusatory tone Maude used, "What do you mean? Are you talking about Moses, Ben and Problem Child?"

"Whatever their names are." Maude huffed, "You don't need to spend so much time at their table. People are starting to talk."

Red wanted to defend herself and explain that they were just friends, but she tensed at the idea that she *HAD* to explain herself. It seemed it was alright if she was very friendly with the white customers, and she had never been called out for spending too much time at a table full of white men. "Let them talk." Red sniffed and started to walk away.

Surprisingly, Maude gripped her by the elbow, "I am saying this for your own good. Wayne asked me to speak to you about this."

Wayne was their manager. Until this very moment, Red, Wayne and Maude had always gotten along well. Red had never been in any trouble at the diner. Even though Maude tried to tone down how she spoke to Red, they both knew this was a verbal warning.

After that verbal warning Red was as nice to Ben and his friends each and every time they came into the greasy spoon, and she spent the same amount of time at their table as she did every table. She still smiled and joked, but she sang less. One thing Red was known for was humming or singing with the juke box if a favorite tune came on. And Ben noticed that she wasn't acting herself.

One night he went to the jukebox and put the coins in to select a song he had heard Red sing along with many times before. This night, Red didn't sing. She smiled and served them and made casual conversation, but she didn't hum or sing. Even Moses noticed the difference.

"Hey, Red." Moses called out, "This is one of your songs, ain't it?"

Red paused behind the counter, tilted her head and gave a weak smile. She glanced at Maude who was watching from the kitchen. "Yes, Moses, I like this song." Any other time Red might have sang a verse. But not tonight.

"It's one of our favorites too." Ben suggested, carrying his money to the register where he watched everyone carefully, every-one who was behind the counter that is. Perhaps he picked up on something, as he gave a slight nod to Maude. Perhaps it was her reaction to his acknowledgement that confirmed his thoughts, because Maude quickly dropped her eyes and turned away from him, but not until she shot Red a crisp look.

Ben slid some coins towards Red across the counter top, "I will be seeing you soon, Red." And he gave a wave to his friends as he departed.

Problem Child motioned for Red to come over. She refilled his coffee as he asked, "Is everything alright with you, Red?"

Again, she looked for Maude, and again she found Maude watching. "Yeah, everything is alright. Some troubles here and there but how is that any different?" Her eyes lingered a moment longer at his concern.

"You know if you need anything, all you have to do is ask." Moses chimed in. Red instinctively patted Moses's dark hand as he slid the money across the table top to her, she had done it many times before, patting the tops of people's hands, and this was her way of acknowledging his kindness.

After the Diner closed Maude and Wayne waited together for Red to finish her closing procedures, and then they asked her to Wayne's office.

Red had a sinking sensation in the pit of her stomach. She needed this job, she had finally caught her rent up and was able to put a few dollars back each week in her secret stash for getting out of her marriage. She hoped her job was secure, but somehow she knew it wasn't.

Maude started out by saying, "Red, you know I've had to talk to you before about fraternizing with those blacks?"

Red looked at Maude then at Wayne, "They are my customers, and they are good customers."

"You sure do give them special treatment." Maude said, "Always finding a reason to touch them." She spat, allowing her words and accusations to sink in.

"Giving out your phone number to customers goes beyond your duties as a waitress." Wayne bellowed and leaned forward, his big belly pushing some of the clutter from his desk.

Maude scurried to pick up the papers that had fluttered to the floor. Red just looked him coolly in the eyes.

Wayne gave a snort, "What, you thought I wouldn't be told about it?" He challenged.

Red pulled in her breath, trying to remain calm. She had given Ben her telephone number a couple of days prior, but not for the reason Wayne accused her of. But she didn't waste her time denying it, why should she?

Wayne shook his head at her, "Customers are saying things that can hurt your reputation and ours."

Red bristled, "I gave Ben my phone number because he has a brother who works on cars, and my car needs some brakes, and I asked that his brother call me."

"So you think his brother, who is a mechanic, should call you instead of you calling him for his service?" Wayne asked and then told Maude, "She must want to get into some sort of mischief with those Negro's."

Maude was nodding in agreement, "Because that doesn't make any sense, Red, since you have a husband who works on cars."

Red felt her spine stiffen, "My husband tinkers with his cars. He is nothing more than a shade tree mechanic." She didn't add that sometimes her own husband deliberately jeopardized her vehicle, in fact, he had once pulled the distributor cap off of her car just to keep her from going to see her parents. " Ralph won't do anything for me if he doesn't get personal gain from it."

Wayne chuckled dryly, "Maybe that's because his wife is out here flirting with all the men and especially the Negro men!"

Before she knew it, Red sprang to her feet.

Maude stepped forward and touched the taller woman's forearm. "Everybody is talking about it. How you flirt and sing to those black men!"

"I smile and sing to most of our regulars!" Red reminded.

"Not in the way you sing to them. All flirty like, twisting your hips and staring at them too long. You know we don't want a bunch of Negro's hanging out in here, making our patrons nervous, and you keep them here just so you can flirt with them." Maude accused.

Red resisted the temptation to slap the smirk off of Maude's face. "I thought you and I were friends." Red seethed.

"I thought you had more class." Maude retorted.

"Ladies!" Wayne boomed with his big voice as he stood up from his rolling office chair.

Both women turned to him, their eyes a little watery. "I don't have all night to listen to a cat fight! You were called into my office with Maude as my witness to be written up for your behavior!" He had already filled out the little yellow form and was sliding it across the table towards Red.

She looked at him and at the paper and wiped a single tear from her eye. She had never been written up before. "This isn't fair." She spoke softly. Moving towards the desk just enough to read what he had written. Her face colored with shame. "What if I refuse to sign it?"

Wayne reared back and grinned one of the cruelest grins Red had ever seen, "Then you will be signing your walking papers tonight."

Red hated the tears that fell from her eyes, betraying herself, showing him her weakness. And she hated the way his grin made her feel. But the anger at the injustice of it all rose up and even though she knew she was sealing her fate she told them, "I reckon some of you can talk out of both sides of your face, and can treat the people you think are beneath you like dirt, but I am not made from that mold! I think we are all humans and we all deserve to be treated with respect and if that means you fire me for treating black men the same as white men then I guess I will be getting my walking papers! Because I refuse to treat them any differently." Red was already untying her apron strings as she saw him pull the yellow paper towards him and as she was slipping the diner key from her key ring she saw that the pink slip had already been written, just in case, and he slid it forward.

She looked deep in his cold gray eyes and dropped the key in his chubby palm. She signed the termination paper and turned and looked at Maude, a slightly older woman whom she had once considered a friend, who had agreed to help get Red's young daughter hired there, who had given her a ride several times in the past when Red's car wouldn't start. And most importantly, someone she had confided in when times became too difficult, just as they had become, and whom she knew was the only person who saw her exchange her telephone number with Ben a few nights prior. "I know who the two faced, split tongued snake is in this diner, for your information, and I won't forget this."

She left Maude and Wayne in silence, although Red knew she was the topic of conversation for days to come.

She didn't bother telling Ralph she had been fired, he would have made it her fault whether or not it was. He had always accused her of *"screwing"* her bosses or any man she appeared to be friendly with. But Red recognized this was his way of turning the attention away from his own philandering's. She had heard about his alleged affair with a woman he worked with. That woman's husband had actually come to the diner to tell Red about it when Ralph and Nadine were caught in a back room engaging in intercourse, both were let go from their positions at work. But Ralph neglected to tell his wife the reason, so she felt she didn't owe him an explanation about her job loss. Red had heard about other affairs, after all she worked with the public and in a small town rumors circulated fast, but Red wasn't jealous. She had stopped caring too many years ago, and besides she kept hoping he would leave her one day for one of the women he cheated on her with. She was never lucky enough for that to happen.

As for Maude, she called Red's house a few days later and told Ralph, who was home at the time, explaining to him that they wouldn't be needing their daughter Evelyn anymore at the diner. When Red got home that day Ralph met her at the door, grabbing her roughly by both wrists, "Why didn't you tell me you got fired for flirting with a Negro?" But he was using the nasty version of the word. "Have you been *screwing* him these past few days, pretending to go to work?"

Red tried to pull her wrists free from his grasp, which only made him twist and squeeze harder, "I haven't pretended to go to work, I have been going out to look for a job, but it seems my reputation has preceded me everywhere I go because they already know I was fired for being too friendly to the black men who came into the diner!!!" She screamed in his face and before she thought better of it she spat in it too. The look of shock that lifted his brows and widened his eyes made Red that much more satisfied with her actions. She wrung her hands free and turned on heel to walk away from the man she had come to loathe.

Days passed with Red driving to the outskirts of Maple Ridge each day to search for a job since it seemed every diner and restaurant in town knew she was overly friendly with the blacks, as if it was a crime to be nice to someone with dark skin. Ben and Moses had noticed her absence at the greasy spoon, but no one was forthcoming with the fact she had been fired.

Ben had resisted calling her home number, he knew she had an unhappy marriage, but he risked it anyway. Her husband answered, and Ben asked for Red.

There was a long pause, "Red's not here. Who is this anyway?" Ralph demanded.

"She works at the greasy spoon and I was hoping you could give her a message, it's very important."

Ben could hear Ralph breathing into the mouthpiece, he could imagine the gears turning as the man calculated a response, Ben could hear Ralph pull in his breath through his nostrils, and "I guess you haven't heard, Red doesn't work at the diner anymore." And Ralph hung up the phone.

Ben held his own phone in his hand for a moment. It sure sounded like things had taken a turn for the worse for Red. He decided to call back, he had dealt with many insecure white men before, and when Ralph answered Ben jumped right in, as if their conversation had never ended, "You would be wrong about that, sir, this call is about a new job. Will you give Red this message, with my number? Tell her she has a job waiting for her if she gets back with me." He didn't pause long enough for Ralph to comment, "But time is of the importance, do you have a pencil handy?"

And that's how he located Red. When she called him back later that day he asked what had happened. Red didn't want him to know that she had been fired for being too friendly to the black customers, so she fibbed a little, "They let me go at the greasy spoon. I didn't have a way to let you and Moses and the others know." Although she had given him her number, he had not given her his. Ben didn't have a phone. He was rarely home, so he used pay phones, his mother's or his brother's phone when he had to.

Red was happy to hear from Ben, but she was disappointed that the call was not about a real job. Money was tight and she feared falling behind again. "Ben, I can't find work around town, I guess Maude and Wayne has told everyone that they fired me."

"Don't worry about it. Tell you what, come over to my Mothers tomorrow for lunch. Tell your husband it's about the job. We

56

will figure something out." He gave Red the address. She had no idea what he or his mother could do to help her get a job, but the matter of fact way he spoke left her feeling hopeful.

That's how Red ended up driving to the 'black side' of town, as was the moniker of this area. She almost chuckled inside as she navigated her way into the section of town that had earned the label of being impoverished and mostly black. She knew she stood out with her pale complexion and bright red hair, yet she didn't feel frightened. She had heard so many stories about drugs and shootings and how the police didn't want to respond to calls out there in *'that'* community. When she drove by the houses they weren't much different from where and how she had lived her entire life. The houses were small, cheap in comparison to a lot of homes, many houses needed repair, but she didn't see any particular thing that made her think it was a bad area of town.

When Ben and his mother received her, Ella made her feel right at home. Ella was a small, loveable woman with a big smile and hugs waiting for Ben's friend, whom she had heard so much about. The house smelled of delicious food. Ben's two brothers were there, Lamont and Dom resembled Ben, though theirs was a lighter complexion. Everyone treated Red as if they had known her forever.

As she sat and ate with the family she learned that Dom and Lamont operated a small gas station and auto repair shop just inside the Wheat community. Exactly as Ben had explained, Dom was the mechanic while Lamont ran the gas station. Ben's mother occasionally picked up sewing jobs as she was a fabulous seamstress, but she was retired. Ben's family had moved to East Tennessee soon after Ben had relocated. For the first time since knowing Ben, Red finally asked, "So what do you do for a living, Ben?"

"I am a janitor at the elementary school."

"I bet that's better than working for that nasty ole Judge!" Ella laughed and they all joined in the laughter. It was refreshing to see that this family has stood by one another, and knew each other so well that they could laugh at the unfortunate circumstances of their lives, and it appeared they didn't keep secrets.

"Speaking of jobs, "Ben broke into the laughter, "Red is in need of one. I was wondering if Terrence might know of anything." And he explained that Terrence was the kitchen manager at the local country club.

Lamont suggested they give him a call. And by day's end, Red was being interviewed by Terrence and his supervisor Avery at the West Side Country Club. Terrence simply asked, "Can you operate a grill?" That's all he needed to know. It didn't matter to him why she was fired, this was entirely a different environment, and Red wouldn't be waiting tables at the country club. In fact, none of the kitchen staff ever went into the dining room or bar area during operating hours. "Mostly snobs come here, they don't want to see the faces of the poor. We can't afford a membership here anyway." Terrence laughed kindly.

The waiters and waitresses wore nicer uniforms than any place Red had previously worked, and they rarely came into the actual working area of the kitchen, which was mostly staffed with minorities, while the dining room was staffed entirely of white people. The servers came to a window to pick up the food, barely speaking with those who worked in the actual kitchen, so it felt as if the snobbery extended to much of the staff as well as the customer base.

Although Red would work the grill, she still had a pretty nice looking uniform. SO when she returned home with uniform in hand, Ralph looked her up and down, searching for a reason to complain. "What did you have to do to get a job at the country club?" His tone was accusatory.

Red showed indifference. She had seen how true friends and family treated each other. She was more determined than ever to find a way out of her marriage.

While she worked at the country club in the kitchen she didn't see Ben or his friends. They definitely weren't privileged enough to be a member of the country club, but Terrence was friends with Ben's family so she asked often about Ella and Ben.

One day a few months into her job, Red's car wouldn't start, as would happen occasionally, and Red placed a call through to Ella for Dom or Ben to call her at the country club. She placed a call to Terrence next, he arranged for a coworker to pick her up so that she wouldn't have to miss work. When Ben called she explained what was wrong and Ben told her that he and Dom would stop by later in the day to get the car keys. She met them at the back door of the kitchen and gave them her address. "When I left, Ralph wasn't home, but if I can catch him I will let him know that you two will stop by and get the car."

Ben and Dom exchanged looks, "Let us worry about him if he is even at home, we may have to tow it, but we will let you know by the end of day."

Red thanked them, "I am so glad you can help me out. Ralph would take too much time if he ever would get around to taking a look at my car."

But in fact, Ralph would be home when Ben and Dom arrived, they didn't bother knocking on his door. The car was parked street side so they used the keys and unlocked the car, gave the ignition a turn then popped the hood and began looking at the engine.

Ralph was completely unaware that two black men had driven up and were inside his wife's car. He was napping through most of it, until one of the neighbors gave his phone a ring that is. That's when and how Ralph met Ben and Dom.

No one ever said Ralph was a brave man, but it didn't mean he was a smart man, either. He went outside and strode over to the two men with hands in trouser pockets. "What do you think you're doing?" He asked in a meek manner.

Ben turned to Ralph, wiping his hands on a shop towel, "Red's car wouldn't start, so she hired us to take a look at it."

"Hired you?" Ralph bounced, "What's she going to pay with? Red don't have any money."

Ben exchanged looks with Dom who was stepping up to the conversation, Dom explained, "We will give her a quote before any work is done to be sure it fits her budget, at first glance it seems simple enough."

Ralph peered at them through judgmental eyes, "Well I reckon if you people even get a nickel you feel like you're rich." He removed his hands from his pocket and turned towards the car, leaning over the hood while peering down at the engine, "Probably the alternator. I can fix that. We don't have the money to pay you people to fix this car, anyway, especially if I can do the work myself."

Dom was first to respond, "Red called us and asked that we take a look. And that's what we are going to do." Dom stated as he approached Ralph with an assured stride, holding out Red's keys in his palm, "Now if you don't mind." He closed the hood and turned to Ben, "Let's hook her up."

Ben strode past Ralph, looking him firmly in the eyes, "Don't worry, we will handle it from here."

Ralph watched in agitation as the two men loaded his wife's car onto the tattered tow truck. He stomped back to the small house they rented and waited until Red returned home. Indeed driving her car, indicating she had paid the colored men to fix it. As soon as she unlocked the front door Ralph jumped her, almost hanging onto her back as he had hidden behind the door in wait. He held her from behind, his hands clawing into her flesh. "I met your two negro friends." He seethed between clenched teeth.

Red bucked at his arms, but he was holding tightly, hurting her abdomen as he squeezed.

He continued speaking, "What did you do, suck their black dicks for the car tow and repair?"

Without thought Red lunged backwards, her head smashing into his chin as their bodies hit the wall in the foyer. "Let me go!" She screamed.

Ralph lost his grip and Red spun around on him, grabbing his neck with both of her hands, squeezing with all of her angry strength.

Ralph's face was red and his eyes wide with surprise and fear and Red watched his eyes began to tear up. And then she heard a small voice from behind her, and felt the tug on her uniform sleeve, "Mommy, what are you doing?" and then the youngest of her children begged, "Please let go of Daddy."

Red loosened her grip but didn't let go immediately and for a moment she wanted to tell the sorry bastard that it was over, because she knew if she didn't leave him for good that one day she might finish choking him to death she hated him so much. But her child had seen too much already so she loosened her grip from around his neck and let him go, turning to find that not only was her youngest child standing there, but the next oldest was now approaching the scene.

That night would mark the beginning of the end of their marriage. Somehow Red managed to keep her anger in check, she nor Ralph spoke to each other that night. And the next morning after she saw her children off to school she warned Ralph, "Don't you ever lay your hands on me again."

Red didn't have enough money to leave him yet, but she worked hard to save what she could and in the meantime she checked for financial aid with help getting an apartment for her and her children. Within a few weeks Red was accepted to live in one of the apartments in a town just outside of Maple Ridge, she would be living in the housing projects, but at this point she would be solely responsible for her finances and children and she wouldn't have to worry about Ralph stealing money from her.

Ralph had taken a temporary job, mostly working 3 days a week, so Red waited for the perfect day when Ralph would be away from home. She had already spoken with Ben and asked if he could help move her within a 5-6 hour period. The day arrived and Ben and four of his friends drove to the house she and Ralph rented. She left Ralph a single bed, and one chair. The team of friends loaded her scant belongings into two pick-up trucks the day Red left Ralph. It was one trip, one effort and just like that Ralph came home to an empty house.

This started the madness that would become Red's life, and by association, Ben's life. Their troubles would be constant and their determination would become their strength. Neighbors of Ralph told him that Red had ran off with a bunch of Negro's. No one knew where she had went, and it would be several days before Ralph located her, but he knew where she worked and soon he waited after work one day to follow her home. There, in front of her recently rented apartment, and any neighbor within ear shot or sight, Ralph confronted her in the street when she and their two youngest children got out of the car.

He was yelling at the top of his lungs, calling her a slut, a dumb bitch and a negro lover and threatening to hurt the man who had caused his wife to leave him, even adding this cutting remark, "You give a colored man an inch and he will take a mile and this is proof because the bastard took my wife!"

Red looked at him firmly, "If you want to see the man who caused me to leave, then take a look in the mirror." She tried to ignore him, she tried to walk the children inside before too many neighbors saw, but Ralph yelled and ranted all the way to her front door where she locked him out. Needless to say he pounded on the door, which resulted in a neighbor calling the police. It would be the first of dozens of visits from the city police department, and Red would score a sour reputation from that moment forward as Ralph loudly told his version of the story, how his wife had taken his children from him and had taken everything they owned and moved out without even a warning or leaving a note, how she had left him for a black man and how broke he was, "She didn't even leave any food in the house." He told them.

The officers cast negative looks in Red's direction, but didn't say much that first time, other than telling Ralph to leave peacefully and suggested he get an attorney.

It seemed after that day the usually quiet neighbors kept up with the red haired lady and her children. Her two oldest children were already working and had moved out of the projects to get away from the hell that was now becoming part of this family's daily routine.

Most evenings when Red came home from work a few of the neighbors would shout at her from their porches, calling her names such as "White Trash!" or worse. Although Ben didn't live with Red, he regularly visited, also mowing her grass, washing her car and visiting often as Red loved to cook home meals for her family and Ben. He and his friends checked on her regularly, they all knew the heated threats that were being made. The neighbors saw this and began spreading rumors. Indicating Red was dating more than one Negro, in fact Red heard that she was dating five black men! It was outrageous how anyone could believe these lies, yet people did and even worse the policemen and firefighters believed it, and most of the officers were as racist as her neighbors.

A couple of the roughest of the women who lived near Red threatened to beat her up, telling her one day they would jump her ass in the dark. Red's children were even bullied in school and harassed in the neighborhood. Red tried to keep them close and keep an eye on them for their safety, but she couldn't be everywhere at every moment.

Her teenage son had even been beaten and tossed around by her male neighbors who were mostly adults themselves, and when the police was called for that disturbance one officer told Red to her face, "The next time we are called out here to your place I won't stop anyone from throwing you and your son in the ditch over there. We don't want your kind dirtying up our city."

Red decided then and there she wouldn't place another call to the local police station asking for help.

It seemed that most of her neighbors hated her and Ben, she couldn't trust even one of them at the time because when Ben was washing her car or mowing her grass some of the male neighbors would cuss at him or call him names as they drove by. But Ben never showed fear and he had instructed Red to never show fear, no matter how much she trembled inside, he told her, "Hate and racism is a disease, and people will feed on fear. They get a mob mentality and follow the crowd and they can get carried away, and that's when something tragic can happen. SO *never* show them you are afraid." He had said to her. "No matter what, stand tall and walk proud and make them wonder why you *aren't* afraid." Red marveled at his strength and courage, even when a few of the men sent word that one day they would "bury that negro in her backyard." Ben came and went from her apartment, appearing confident in the face of fire, which bled over to Red, because she was learning to feel the determination more than the fear.

The housing projects were located near a city park and a hate group known as the Ku Klux Klan were very active during this era, their group held rallies at night in local parks around the area. One weekend the KKK came to Canton, and much of the city's inhabitants attended the rally. A few nights after that some of Red's neighbors erected a wooden cross in her yard and ignited a fire, extending a very clear message that she and her family and especially her Negro friends weren't wanted. That's when the fire department and police showed up again. After the cross was extinguished and things calmed down a fireman told Red, "So this is because you like to date black men? Maybe you should turn back to dating whites and you won't have so much trouble."

Then there was Ralph. Calling with threats frequently. Someone had loosened the wheel lugs on her car one night and Red noticed the bumping sound it made so she eased the car to the side of the road. A nice man stopped to help her and told her that her wheel was loose. What would cause it to be loose, she asked. "About the only thing I can think of is that someone deliberately loosened it." He said. Leaving Red to wonder, was it a neighbor again or was it Ralph? Once he had made the threat that one day she would be coming home around the river road on the way home from work and she would end up in that river. She called him later that night and accused him of loosening the lugs and she reminded him that they had children and the children rode in her car to school, "What if I had wrecked and killed our children?"

"You brought this on yourself." He told her and hung up.

Another morning she woke up to discover that the driver's side window on her automobile had been busted out by a rock with a note wrapped around it reading, "Go away, white trash!"

During these times Ben taught Red how to keep tough through it all. He walked with pride everywhere they went, he never showed anger or rage, even though Red could see in his eyes and from the way his jaw was held firmly in place that he was prepared to protect himself, and would protect Red and her children.

One weekend Red received a call at the country club and someone told her, "When you come home tonight and turn that doorknob, you and your children will be blown straight into hell."

Red didn't have any faith in the police officers anymore and so she called Ella, once again asking for Ben to call her at work. She told Ella what had happened and the sweet woman told her, "Bring those children to my house and stay a few nights here until it all cools down. Ben will be in touch in a little while." Red knew he would, he had never let her down. Admittedly, Ben had become her pillar of strength.

When Ben called, Ella had already filled him in on the latest threat and he told Red, "Don't you worry. I want you to go to Mother's and stay until the weekend. I and some of my friends will make sure your apartment is safe." And just like that he found several of his friends who went with him the next day to check on the apartment. The neighbors may have thought they had scared Red enough to stay away when she didn't come home that first night. But when three black men went to her apartment, and checked inside, then proceeded to stay in the apartment in shifts around the clock, the neighbors seemed to realize they weren't scaring this family away.

Perhaps the neighbors had successfully ran some families off, because Red had lived there long enough to see them gang up on certain families, even physically fighting them on their front lawns. The one other black family was ran off and a single woman with her son was also beat up and ran off. But Red stayed. Not because she wanted to, no, she hated living there. But because she wouldn't let racism run her or Ben off. They were going to fight back.

She and Ben and Ella went to the police department the next day after her car window was broken, taking the hand written note with them, and they demanded a report be made, "In case we need to have a report handy." Red told them.

Ella, being the sweet, elderly woman she was, even told the cop at the desk in a polite yet direct manner, "This has gone on long enough! And if this town won't help put a stop to it, we will!"

Ella wrote a letter to the editor of the local newspaper, detailing what had happened with the cross burning, the threats, the teenaged son being attacked and the broken car window incident and she even threw in the car wheel being loosened. A news reporter from the local television station in a larger bordering town contacted Ella, who pointed them to Red and she was interviewed. The journalist did an unbiased interview and reported the story fairly, which may have been the first time in Red's and Ben's life that someone actually did something favorable. It aired one late night during the last part of the 11pm news. Soon thereafter a few more families in the surrounding towns in the viewing area of this television station came forward with their own stories. Finally, the secret was out, the little town was polluted with prejudice and hatred, and the local law enforcement did little to stop it.

Perhaps Ralph read the article or saw the news because he stopped calling his ex-wife with threats. She had hired an attorney and filed for divorce and it was finalized about the same time of the broadcast. Red wasn't sure why he stopped but she didn't even mind that he never paid child support or rarely took visitation with their youngest children, because this meant he was finally out of her life.

The neighbors didn't stop harassing, they just became less violent, although a few of them had moved away over time, and a few of them had become nicer, Red never trusted any of them, they still talked and whispered about Ben and Red behind their backs, but after a time they mostly left them alone.

Ben and Red and her children could even sit outside at night and enjoy their lives. She never thought she would see the day that she could relax outside and share time with her greatest friend.

Red found a manufacturing job in Canton, which paid more and had better benefits and was a few minutes from home. Her son joined the Navy when he turned eighteen. Her youngest child was finally doing better in school. Life was finally looking up and calming down. For Red, this was worth the struggles she had endured.

As for Ben, maybe the calmer life didn't suit him as much as he had thought it would. Maybe he had protected a white, corrupt judge in the earlier days of his life, then protected a white, down on her luck woman in the middle part of his life, but it seemed he wanted to move on, or maybe he simply craved more excitement.

Red began to notice that he had more money to spend than usual. He would take her and the children to movies sometimes, or out to eat at nice restaurants. Red knew as a janitor he couldn't be making that much more money. But when he opened his wallet to pay for their dinners she could see the stack of twenty dollar bills.

Red trusted Ben, yet she questioned him, "Where did you come into all of that money?" She asked one night as they sat on her back porch enjoying a beer.

Ben was honest, as she knew he would be, "I've been playing poker with some friends."

"Poker? You mean, you're gambling again?" It wasn't that she didn't approve, but during their many conversations he had admitted he had left gambling behind when he left Louisiana.

Ben smiled, "Well the truth is I'm much better at Tonk, that's when I win the most."

Red had no idea what Tonk was, but she understood the term poker, "Isn't gambling dangerous, Ben?" Red asked.

Ben paused for a moment, "Is it any more dangerous than driving through a white neighborhood where most of the people hate me for being black?" He saw that his remark didn't sit well with his friend, so he shifted in his seat scooting a little closer and took one of her hands in his, "Don't worry about me, Red. When I sit at that table, I know what cards I'm holding in my hand, I don't play for fun as much as I play for money. I'm all business." He smiled slightly, "If someone wants to get wild and wooly I have protection." He lifted his shirt and showed her his gun, which he had never flaunted or showed her before, no matter how hard times had been. "It's a Saturday Night Special. I know at any given moment I can put my hand on it and its always loaded and ready to fire."

"Have you always had that?" She inquired.

"Of course."

Red didn't push the subject, she respected and trusted Ben, and truth is, she probably even loved him, but she had never told him. After all, life was getting better and she had hoped they would be able to enjoy the calmer times. But just as life had thrown them together, it would also pull them apart.

Red worked overtime regularly, it was mandatory, plus she needed the money. She had a plan. But her hours often kept her away from home and she didn't spend as much time with Ben. Not that Ben and Red didn't stay in touch, he still called and talked to her, and sometimes they met for breakfast on a random Saturday morning. Occasionally she went with him to visit his family, but it seemed the visits grew farther and farther part.

But Red was building her future and soon she found a quaint home near her job and her daughter's school and she made an offer on the house. Red called Ben first when the offer was accepted and he and his brothers again helped her when she moved into the small, older house, this time she wasn't renting it she was buying it! Red had never dreamed she would ever be able to own a house of her own.

She invited Ben. Lamont, Dom and Ella over for a dinner to celebrate and to show them her home. It was a wonderful reunion. They talked long up into the wee morning hours, sharing old stories and catching up on the latest. When everyone was leaving Red gave each of them a tight hug. It would be the last time Red would see Ben alive.

When she got the call she was in utter shock. It was Lamont, when he started talking Red knew something was wrong, "Red, this is Lamont. I have some bad news." She wrongly assumed that it was Ella who had died. Then Lamont said, "Mom has been asking for you, she knows you would want to attend Ben's funeral. But she has been so upset that she couldn't find your number. I came over and found it, and she asked me to call you, she wants you to attend his services tomorrow, and to sit by her side with all of us."

Red was so stunned she couldn't form words to ask what had happened, Lamont gave her the name of the funeral home. She sat and thought about all of the good times and the bad times she had faced with Ben and her heart ached deeply.

The next day she felt privileged to sit with the family and she and her youngest daughter attended his services. When they arrived they were treated warmly, even though they didn't know most of the people there. Red knew Ben's immediate family and a few of his closest friends and that's all that mattered. She sat with Ben's mother and brothers and their wives. Ella patted her hand and spoke softly, "Thank you, Red, you were the closest to a daughter n law for Ben that I ever had."

Red kept the tears inside, her mind reeling in disbelief that Ben was truly gone. The services became a blur to Red, so engrossed in her memories she found herself. Over and over she silently repeated, 'This can't be, Ben can't be gone.'

"I hate to ask, but what happened? Did someone do something to him?"

Ella lifted her eyes to the skies and a small smile tugged at her lips, "Did you hear that, Ben? Red thinks somebody got to you." She looked at the white woman with a deep fondness in her eyes, "Red, there wasn't nobody ever could take Ben down and I am proud to say no one but the good Lord did."

Red's face registered a pleasant surprise. "He just died on his own?"

"Yes he did." Ella confirmed, "Went to sleep and didn't wake up. We found out he had a congenital heart problem not too long ago. It was just his time, Red. It was his time to go."

Both women were smiling through their salty tears, each for the same reason, because Ben had walked through times which few people would have survived, protecting those who mattered while protecting himself. And he never let any one person bring him down. He never let the injustices of life stop him.

This is the story Red wanted to share, the story of Ben, a man of character and the bravest man she had ever known.

The End

Hack

By J. Poore 8/2016

Not everyone is born the same. After all, who expects everyone to be the same? Surely no one, of course! Then WHY do people shun or persecute those who differ?

Everyone knew him. If you came from Brockville, or had ever lived in Brockville for any length of time you knew him. Chances are your parents knew his parents. They probably also knew his grandparents. In small communities it seems everyone knows one another. It's not uncommon for families to live in local towns for generations, hardly anyone leaves their roots in a place like Brockville.

Hack's parents were Gene and Mildred Brooner, Gene worked at the hardware store when he wasn't tending the farm. Hack's grandparents were Sam and Libby Brooner, Sam had inherited the farm through his marriage to Libby Duncan when her parents passed on. It was with pride that Libby and Sam left the farm to Gene in their will. But that generation has since left this world, gone home to be with Jesus.

Harold Brooner, known as "Hack" since he was three years old, was born to a hard working religious couple, who wouldn't miss a church service no matter the day of the week. They had always suspected their firstborn, their only son, was a tad slow from early on, he didn't learn to speak until his second year of life, he didn't start to walk 'til nearly then, but they loved him just the same. And they didn't want him treated any differently than anybody else.

The townspeople knew the Brooner family, most of them liked and respected them, and Hack was treated like any other child for the most part. Except for the bullies and mean-hearted, you can't stop a mean hearted person from being cruel or insensitive. But fortunately for Hack he was loved by many and in cases where he wasn't liked at all, or was bullied, it helped that he wasn't a small boy. It's not to say the bullying and cruel words didn't have an effect on him. In retrospect, it appears it had a very significant effect after all.

Hack weighed over 10 pounds at birth and was an impressive 22 1/2 inches long. As he grew he towered above most of his peers and outweighed most of them considerably. He wasn't obese, especially not after he outgrew his "baby fat", as his Mamma liked to call it.

"We have to make that boy work." Gene would tell Mildred, because Mildred had a tendency to try to over protect him, and 'baby' him too much.

"You don't need to be so hard on that boy, Gene." Mildred often scolded, especially when she felt that Gene pushed Hack too hard.

"I'm not hard on him. We both know he's a little slow with his learning, and his smarts sure won't get him through this life. He's gonna have to develop some sort of skill and a lot of muscle to defend himself, and besides, he needs to work some of that fat off." Gene would say time and again.

"That's just baby fat." Mildred stated, even when Hack was ten years old, when the boy was already a head taller than her and outweighed her by 25 pounds. "He will lose his baby fat soon enough."

And he did. In fact, Hack wasn't an overweight, blubbery person; he was as solid as a rock and fairly good with his hands. From his first day at school until his last day, Hack was a teacher's favorite because he was physically big enough to help them move furniture and lift heavy things when needed and he was mentally eager enough to want to please his teachers.

When Hack spoke it was slow and deliberate, as if he had to think before he put words together, but he could "converse" with anyone, the fact remained that he just chose not to "converse" a lot.

Maybe his silence disturbed some people and maybe that's why some of the more mischievous children, and even some narrow minded grown-ups thought it was alright to make fun of him. He never graduated from high school, he dropped out in the tenth grade, and he was already 18 years old by then. His father had died unexpectedly from a massive heart attack that same year and he knew his Momma needed him to man up, and to help her take care of the farm so he quit school much to her disappointment. In fact, Hack preferred the farm life to school. On the farm he labored hard and didn't have to always defend or prove himself, on the farm he was adequate.

His Momma slipped into a depression and wanted to sell the farm, but Hack refused to listen to her reasoning. "We can keep the farm, Momma. Together we can work it and keep the bills paid." He spoke slow and steady and sure of himself as he had given much thought to their situation.

But Mildred knew that as she aged Hack wouldn't be able to keep up with the farm work by himself. She wouldn't be able to keep working at the same pace for very much longer, either. One person couldn't run the farm. She wondered if Hack would every get married. He had never had a girlfriend. He liked a few of the girls in school, but none returned the sentiment.

"It's too much, Hack. The old Duncan farm is too big for just you." They had twenty acres, with a small portion of it backing up to the river. They had cattle, pigs, chickens, a big garden, they had always sold their fruits and vegetable at the farmer's market on weekends. That farm and their old house was all they had, and it had been in the family for a few generations, but it looked like the family tree was stopping with Hack.

Sadly, Mildred's brother Thomas was killed on a farming tractor when it tipped over and crushed him. He was married but hadn't fathered any children. And Gene had a sister who died from spinal bifida at age 4. Gene and Mildred had tried to have more children, in fact, Mildred had been pregnant three other times but always miscarried. Hack was the end of their heritage if he failed to find a wife and make a baby, especially a son.

By the time Hack was 23 years old Mildred had already sold almost all of the cattle. They kept two cows and they always kept one or two pigs, and half a dozen chickens. This was the year she sold half of the acreage.

"I have to sell it, Hack." She tried to explain, but he refused to listen. In fact, he had become so agitated that his behavior had startled Mildred. His behavior had rattled her so much that the next Sunday after church she mentioned to the pastor how Hack would pace back and forth, clinching and unclenching his fists, giving her hard looks anytime she said or did anything he didn't like. During these times she missed Gene the most, his stern, fatherly ways which she complained about during Hack's early childhood could have ended this unexpected and unappreciated display of anger and frustration.

"I think Hack feels worthless. " The pastor told her, "I think he feels like a failure. Maybe we need to find him some work outside of your farm work. "

"Pastor George, Hack has no special skill, nobody would hire him." It was the first time that Mildred had ever said this, and she dropped her head in shame, more so ashamed of herself than of her son.

"He has a lot of skill, Mildred. He has big hands and a strong back and a mind good enough to follow directions. Let's start here, at the church he grew up in and loves so well. We need some things done around the lawn and a lot of clean up at the cemetery. I will have the men show him how to do some things and we will pay him for it. Remember, God always provides a way, and this is God's house."

When the pastor hired Hack to help some of the men with cleaning up the cemetery, and eventually doing some landscaping Hack felt a pride he had never known. Before long he even helped dig the graves, he could operate heavy machinery after they showed him how.

Mildred was very proud and she knew that Gene was smiling from the heavens. Hack was earning a small income, helping her pay some bills around the house, while keeping up with their garden. But the house really needed some repairs.

Again Mildred spoke to the Pastor, and he again offered similar advice. "Hack is one of the hardest workers I have ever known. And some of the members of our church have hired Hack to help them out with little odd jobs from time to time. I think it's time we let him earn a living wage and maybe it's time you sell off a little more land and maybe the cows or pig so you can have the money to buy the things you need for the house-hold repairs."

Much to hers and Hack's sadness Mildred sold another 5 acres of the land. She only kept a few chickens and 1 pig, which after this pig was slaughtered she would be done with the livestock. Their garden was once again downsized and essentially they ate from the garden, there wasn't much leftover to sell at the farmer's market.

The family who bought the 5 acres pulled a trailer onto the land, and they had a daughter who had just turned 18. Hack was 25 years old. He liked Marjorie, and at first she seemed friendly enough.

But soon she grew tired of his constant visits and lost the patience to listen to his awkward efforts to make conversation. Hack didn't recognize that some of her sarcastic remarks were mean spirited. He didn't recognize that her excuses to get away from him were blatant lies. Mildred could see through her, and she disliked the girl. She knew that Hack was being set up for heartache.

Sometimes a mother predicts things she would rather not, and true to Mildred's worry, Marjorie began to spread lies about Hack, saying unkind things about him to anyone who leant an ear. One such rumor was that Hack would fondle himself sometimes when he spoke to her. Mildred knew better than this, she sometimes watched them talking to each other from her secure spot at the kitchen window, and sure Hack fidgeted a lot and pulled his pants up by the belt loop but he had never once touched himself inappropriately.

Mildred tried to warn Hack of Marjorie, telling him that if she wasn't interested in friendly conversation or to be a friend not to take it too personally, and to walk away. But Hack had fond feelings for the sandy haired girl and each evening he brought her an apple or a peach or even a flower from the lower field.

Then it happened, one day Hack came storming home, slamming the door so hard it rattled the windows. Mildred tried to ask him what was wrong, but he wouldn't speak. He went out back to the stump where he would chop wood just like his father always had done, and he chopped wood until it got too dark to see. Then he went to the river to "think", this is what he told his Mother, not returning until after midnight.

For nearly a week he departed home early and returned late and didn't speak to his mother beyond a grunt. Mildred did some asking around and snooping and was briefly relieved to discover that Hack had been working with some local men building a handicap ramp at the library. They had also been stopping by the bar after they finished each evening to have a few beers. This particular revelation didn't sit well with Mildred, but the cashier at the grocery store told her Hack was safe, "Bill works with Hack and he watches out that Hack only has 1 beer, and he won't let Hack get into any trouble." She promised; Bill was her husband.

"Has Bill mentioned anything about the girl Hack has a crush on?" Mildred inquired.

"No." The woman hadn't heard anything about that.

But at church the following Sunday Mrs. Marlow had, and she was eager to tell Mildred all about it. "Hack tried to kiss her." Mrs. Marlow said and the look on her face mirrored Mildred's which was pure disbelief. "And she slapped him for it! She told him to leave her alone and never speak to her again!"

Words were lost upon Mildred, but when she finally found her voice she asked the woman, "Marjorie slapped Hack?"

"That's what she told Linda, and I believe what Linda tells me." Linda was another church member.

Mildred felt her cheeks flush, did everyone know about this? She rushed to her pastor and once again confided her worries. Her face a mask of worry and seriousness, in that it drew her brows together and deepened the crevices in her aging face, "I wish Gene was still here to talk to our boy! I don't know how to talk to him about these things."

The pastor said he would have a little man to man talk with Hack. He had always liked Hack since he was a little boy, he could see that Hack wanted to be obedient and wished to be liked. But he could also see something else, something that unnerved him a little bit, and it was the same thing Mildred saw, there was something about Hack that made one worry if he ever truly lost his temper…such thoughts were whisked away by the mind, but those thoughts left a trail of concern in their wake.

When the Pastor spoke to Hack, the young man seemed to want to ask questions. "Hack, I know you are a good soul, and you know you are a good man as well as I know it. But not everyone is good like that. Some folk don't even know how to be good people. But you do, and I am proud of you."

Hack stepped from right foot to left and back again, much like a child. But he was a man now, at least 6 foot 3 and at least 250 pounds if not more. "But God gets to deal with those people, Hack, we have to forgive them. We can't be Christians and not have forgiveness in our hearts. Do you understand, Hack?"

"Yes, sir, I understand." Hack said in his slow mannerism. "Pastor, uh, what is this about?"

"It's not about one thing, Hack, it's about everything. But, if there was one thing I could bring out of it, would be your little neighbor lady, Marjorie, you know her, some say you are a little sweet on her."

Hack's cheeks flushed and he looked at his pastor, his eyes revealing the words before his mouth could, "I liked her a lot."

Pastor George seized the moment, "You liked her? That's speaking in past tense, so now you *don't* like her?"

Hack answered with all of the innocence of a child, "Not anymore. I don't ever want to see her again."

"Hack, this is the forgiveness we just talked about. Whatever Marjorie did, she has to be forgiven of." He gave the young man a moment to ponder, "Sometimes women don't realize how easily they can hurt a man's heart."

Hack lifted a finger to his own cheek and laid it there, "She also hurt my face when she slapped it."

"Well now, she shouldn't have struck you, that's for sure!" The pastor mused, "Why did she hit you?"

Hack shrugged his shoulders.

"Did you do or say something right before she slapped you?"

Hack nodded and again shifted from foot to foot, "I asked her to go on a date with me."

"That's no reason to slap you, Hack. She could have said a simple 'no'. You would understand if she didn't want to date you that maybe she only likes you for a friend, maybe she is sweet on somebody else, maybe she doesn't want a sweetheart at all, different people have different reasons for wanting things different from *what we* want." The Pastor was trying to be as simple as he could be.

Hack looked at the floor before saying, "Why would she hate me? She said she hated me and that I made her feel sick."

Pastor George felt sorrow tug at his heart, that was a very unkind thing for the young woman to say to someone so simple, "I can't answer that, Hack, because as I told you sometimes people are unkind, or hard hearted or they just don't know how hurtful they can be with their words."

"She knew she would hurt me when she slapped me." Hack said matter of fact.

"Indeed she did." The Pastor reluctantly agreed. "May I tell you something, Hack? It's something I figure you already know, but in case you are unsure about it, keep in mind that you can't force yourself on a woman, or on anyone. In other words, you can be kind and sweet and you sure can ask a lady for a date, but you can't just reach out and hold her hand unless she gives you a signal that it's alright, and you can't hold her in your arms until she wants you to, and you can't kiss her until she kisses you first, and not every girl is the same, so some girls will not want you to do any of those things for a long time."

Hack was silent for a moment, finally he said, "I know that, Pastor, and I didn't try any of those things." From the look on his face, Hack was speaking the truth, "Marjorie told me that she bet I wanted to kiss her and touch her and when I said I did she started laughing at me and said she wouldn't let me kiss her ass." Hack's cheeks flushed again, probably because he was swearing right in front of his pastor. But in a faster momentum, yet slower than the average person at confession Hack said, "And she showed me her ass right then, just bent over and raised her dress and said she wouldn't let me kiss her ass, and she ran off laughing at me!"

"When you asked her on a date she bent over and mooned you?" Pastor George asked.

"No, when I asked her for a date she slapped me. She mooned me before that."

The Pastor was the one who was momentarily silenced and he dropped his gaze to the floor. He wished he knew more than he did about this Marjorie person, but her family wasn't in church, not that he was aware of. "Hack, what kind of a girl moons a young man and says something like that?"

"Marjorie is the kind of girl who does that." Hack stated as pointedly as he could.

"Didn't that make you *not* want to ask her for a date?"

This is when Hack's face colored a deep red and his eyes darted back and forth across the older man's face.

Pastor George realized then that there was a lot more to this story, but he didn't know how to approach the subject, "Did that make you want to date her even more? Hack, man can be weakened by the sight of a pretty woman's flesh and that isn't abnormal, but a man has to control the desire, it is written in the Bible."

Hack studied the pastor in absolute silence, an awkward, lengthy silence. Hack seemed to fidget even more.

"Do you understand, Hack? There is nothing wrong with having natural feelings, as long as you don't act on those feelings. In other words…"

"I didn't act on any feelings." He said in a stern and deepened voice, "If I would have acted how I felt I would have picked her up and crushed her when she slapped me!"

Pastor George's mouth gaped as his eyes widened, but he recovered his voice quickly, because he could sense that Hack was ready to turn on heel and storm away, "Thank the Lord you didn't do that. Thank the Lord, Hack, because deep inside you are a good person. And the Lord looks favorably upon those who are obedient to His laws."

Hack was breathing heavily and his brows were knitted, he gave the pastor a curt nod.

"I hope you know that if you ever need to talk to me or have any questions that I am available for you." The Pastor reminded and

Hack gave another short nod and turned away, leaving the Pastor with a knotted feeling deep inside.

After that day Hack avoided Marjorie like the plague, if he saw her he changed his direction if he was walking, and for this Mildred was relieved. The Pastor confirmed he had spoken with Hack and also told her that Hack had said Marjorie slapped him after he asked her for a date. This made Mildred despise the young woman even more.

One day Mildred was at the post office and Marjorie was there as well. Marjorie looked at Mildred with visible disdain. Perhaps it was reflected back to her, because Mildred didn't have a face that hid her feelings well. But Mildred was a polite, well raised woman, so she tightened her lips in a thin grimace determined not to say a word to the girl. But as fate would have it, Mildred's attempt at turning the other cheek only lasted until she finished her postal business. When she turned around from the front clerk there stood Marjorie right upon her heels and the young female snickered, "Aren't you Hack's mother?"

"Yes I am." Mildred tilted her chin up, tossing her head back with pure pride, "And I know who you are."

Again a sarcastic snicker, "I bet you do." Marjorie's voice dripped with taunting. "Would you care to give Hack a message from me?"

"I would care, indeed. I think it's best that the two of you forget that you even know each other." Mildred snorted.

Marjorie wasn't to be deterred from the message she intended to give, but "message" was a kind version, it was more of threat than a message, "That would be easy if your weird son would stop stalking me and watching me through my windows." She paused to allow the accusation to color Mildred's cheeks, then she resumed with a confidence older than her actual maturity, "If he keeps doing that after you give him my message, my Daddy says his ass will be grass, my Daddy is getting sick and tired of it and so am I." Marjorie flipped her hair over her shoulder and strode up to the postal desk to do whatever she came to do, leaving Mildred shocked and embarrassed.

But a protective mother never turns her back on her child, so Mildred walked ever so slowly out of the post office, stopping in wait on the sidewalk in front of the building. When Marjorie came outside it was the younger woman who showed surprise this time as Mildred walked deliberately up to Marjorie, standing face to face, "I've decided I will give Hack your message, which I don't believe a word of it, however I have a message of my own for your precious Daddy. If he lays one finger on my son I will blow him into hell with my 12 gauge shotgun and you better believe I mean it." Unlike Marjorie, Mildred did not turn on heel and walk away, she stood firm and determined until the younger woman stuttered and stammered and backed away, finally hastening her pace to get out of the presence of Mildred Brooner.

When Hack returned home that evening Mildred was very anxious to speak to him about her encounter with Marjorie at the post office and she delivered the ensuing messages. Hack's face turned a deep red when Mildred told him what she and Marjorie had said to each other.

This subconscious reaction disappointed Mildred as she assumed he was guilty as charged, and her shoulders stooped on the exhalation of a sigh, "Harold Brooner, I never would have thought you would lower yourself to stalk any woman or watch her through her window."

This seemed to anger Hack even more as he began to shift his weight and clench his teeth so hard Mildred could hear them grind. Mildred was beside herself with despair and worry and retreated to her room.

It always bothered Hack when his mother called him by his given name, she never used it unless she was angry with him, and although she seemed angry she also seemed very disappointed with him.

His muscles tensed and his arms ached to release the tension. His mind grasped for something to help soothe the growing agitation. There wasn't any more wood for Hack to chop, he loved to use the ax when he felt this way, he enjoyed the raw power from watching his strength and the sharpness of the blade split the wood in two. Hack went to the tool shed and looked at the tools there. His mind firing more rapidly than it usually did. He picked up the scythe and strode heatedly from the shed.

Behind the barn near the edge of the woods, where Hack rarely mowed he began swinging that scythe, clearing a path. A path to where he didn't know or care, it just felt so good to use his muscles and brawn and to see that sharp blade slicing through the waist high grass and weeds and saplings. He could hear critters scrambling to get out of his way and he wished one *would* get in the way, his mind could envision the fur and blood of a creature separating from bone on the curved blade, becoming air born in opposing directions.

Sweat beaded above his upper lip and dripped from his hair into his eyes, blurring his vision, but he wiped the sweat away with his forearm and kept swinging the scythe. Finally he came to the edge of the woods, pausing to look back at the trail he had made. He was pleased with what he had done, even if it had no purpose other than to vent his frustration.

He decided to clear another path back to the barn, still wiping the sweat from his brow, his mind filtering the accusations that had been made about him by the neighbor girl he had crushed on, and his own mother's words *about* him and *to* him. How could *she* believe

Marjorie over him? And then the threat that his "ass will be grass" by anyone, anyone at all made his anger roar like claps of thunder inside the thoughts of his fervent head. The thought of Marjorie's Dad doing anything to him filled him with a deep rage, and a surprising touch of excitement, because if her father was in front of him anywhere in this field he would certainly cut the older man down without any regret or despair, as easily as the weeds sailing on the wind. Hack lifted his eyes to see the trailer where Marjorie and her family lived. He wished they had never moved there.

Her Daddy wasn't even home yet, but soon enough he would be. Her mother was probably watching television, which seemed to be her only hobby.

What was Marjorie doing inside the trailer? He didn't want to know, yet his mind fed him countless possibilities. Some imagined and some he had actually seen for himself. He had not been deliberately spying on her, but how could he help but see her at night when her bedroom was illuminated on the far end and she didn't pull her blinds and the light irradiated the room like a television screen? Sometimes she was just sitting on her bed, or reclining on her bed perhaps feeling bored. Other times she danced to music only she could hear because he was too far away to hear it. And then sometimes, well, every night she peeled her clothes away to slip into her gown. And this was when Hack couldn't look away, no matter how hard he tried.

He knew he wasn't supposed to see her nudity but she so freely exhibited it. And he felt a heated shame each and every time. But Marjorie knew he would be finishing his chores, putting his tools away and feeding the hog. She KNEW this because several times she had stood square in front of the window, looking in his direction as she unhooked her bra and slid it down her arms, twirling it on a forefinger until she flipped it to the floor. And the smile on her face as she looked down at her own breasts, twisting her upper torso with pride and temptation.

Hack wanted to look away, and he almost always did look down or turn from the vision of her, but curiosity always weakened him and in a burning shame he always looked again and in spite of everything he knew was wrong he wanted to see her, to see her breasts and the butt she swore she wouldn't even let him kiss. He wasn't even sure he wanted to kiss it, or kiss her for that matter, because these thoughts of Marjorie both excited him and unnerved him and made him resent her existence even more.

He was swinging the scythe so hard and fast now and the blood pumped through his veins in rhythm with an overworked heart and he stopped in the field, still staring at her trailer. He wished he could bring her to this spot in the field… he wished he could drag her to this spot and could see the look of her eyes wide as he held her against her will, her feet unable to touch the ground as he held her by her thin, milk white neck. A pleasure cooled his burning, hot body as he envisioned what that moment would feel like and in spite of how wrong and evil his thoughts were his mind played it all out for him, in morbid detail he saw himself touching and squeezing her soft, forbidden body… until her breath left her and she would slip greasily from his moist hands onto the freshly cut earth which smelled of green life, unlike her body which would have given up its life in the wake of his revenge.

"Hack!!!!!! Harold Gene *what* are you doing?" His mother yelled from the barn, standing with hands on hips and anger etching her face. She saw her son standing in the field, watching Marjorie's trailer, just as Marjorie had accused.

Hack looked at his mother, hating the screech of her voice and the way she had just screamed both of his names. Hating that she had interrupted his thoughts, because they were all that soothed him, and now the anger was rising, he could feel it building from within.

"You come here right now young man!" She demanded.

Hack studied her. He loved her but he didn't love how she had been treating him. He didn't want to hurt his mother, therefore when she angered him he always got away from her presence. It seemed he needed to get away more often than he ever had. He also knew at this precise moment he did not want to be confronted by her and hear her speech.

He tossed the scythe to the ground, afraid that if he kept it he might do something he would regret. He walked with a long stride towards his mother and watched as her hands fell from her hips. He also watched as her chin dropped open and he took notice as her eyes widened as he approached her without any indication of slowing down. His mother took a few steps backward and she began to mumble something but Hack wasn't listening, his only words were these, "I wasn't doing nothing wrong." And he strode past her, determined to get to the truck and get as far away from his mother and the trailer Marjorie lived in.

Pastor George was surprised when Hack drove up in his driveway. The hulking man got out of his father's truck and strode with purpose and intent toward the porch, where George and his wife Evelyn were enjoying the cool of the evening drinking lemonade. Evelyn looked at her husband quizzically and he motioned her to go inside, which she promptly obliged. The long strides and heavy swing of Hack's arms and his slightly bowed head indicated he was troubled, and his eyes, blazing from beneath a heavy brow never blinked or softened. His boots pronounced his arrival as he stepped heavily onto the wooden stoop.

"Sorry to bother you, Pastor." Hack stated in a rather unapologetic tone. "You said if I ever needed you…"

"Have a seat Hack." Pastor George motioned.

Hack swayed in thought for a moment, shoved his hands deep into his pockets and stood. "I would rather stand." He pronounced.

"Suit yourself. What can I help you with?" The pastor folded his hand over the other across his belly and leaned back in his seat.

"I need to ask for forgiveness. I need for God to help me with some bad feelings I have been feeling."

Pastor George nodded. "Concerning your neighbor Marjorie?"

"Marjorie, and her father, and my mother. I need to be forgiven and I need God to show me how I can stop having bad thoughts."

Surprised, George sucked in his breath, "What kind of bad feelings? Are you angry with your mother and the girl's father for disapproving of your friendship?"

Hack pondered this question for several awkward moments. Finally he said, "I am angry at all of them for making me feel bad, for the things they say and do that make me feel very bad. I have thoughts of hurting them, of making them feel sorry for saying these things."

It was George's turn to leave a gap in their conversation as his mind swirled around the words Hack had just confessed as the young man stood on his porch. Silently he prayed he could say the right thing. "Do you remember the ten commandments, Hack?"

Hack nodded yet shrugged his shoulders, as though he remembered most of them.

"These are the guiding fundamentals of life. If we live by these rules, that is all we need to lead a just life. Remember the commandment to honor thy parents? And to love thy neighbor, and we should not covet thy neighbor? That means we must suppress any feelings of hatred, envy, jealousy or anger. By coming to me and asking for God's help, you are doing the right thing."

Hack didn't falter, he didn't blink, he didn't seem to respond at all, and he simply looked at the pastor. Silently. Awkwardly.

"Hack, you have taken the first step to forgiveness and you can and surely will forgive all three of them for making you feel the bad stirrings, which are as human as nature intended. God created us in His image and He forgives us of every sin. To forgive is God-like. All you need to do is pray when you have these angry emotions, pray and God will answer."

Perhaps Hack understood. Even if he didn't, he accepted the wiser man's advice and from that day forward when he had these feelings he lowered his head in prayer, determined to fight the darkness and the searing heat that cradled a cold heart, a damaged soul which had always teetered on the edge of acceptance, but had never truly been accepted.

He had always heard the snickers, the whispered comments and insults about him, all of his life he had looked straight into the smiling faces, yet heard the cutting remarks behind his back. He hadn't heard them all, but he had heard more than enough. And the voices, disembodied and spoken in the past, but heard in the present, swirled around him daily as he worked with men who had lives and experiences and real things to talk about. Hack heard the echo of voices from his childhood, "Something just isn't right.", "He's sweet enough, but that won't get him far."; "I think he might be a touch retarded.", "He's such a simpleton.", "I don't want him on my team."

And the cutting comments filtered through the real voices, often blurring his reality, and they even filtered through the nice comments he received, these recollections of fragmented conversations were always reminding him of his imperfections. "They call him *Hack* because he had bad asthma attacks when he was young, and coughed up snot and shit like that!", "Those poor old parents wore themselves down trying to get that boy up and grown!", "They should have let him die, instead they rushed him to the hospital every time he had one of those coughing spells!", "Them steroids probably made him so big!" and the girls' favorite, "He is such a goober!"

His coworkers tried to be patient and nice to him, but at the same time they didn't engage with him on the same level as they did each other. They often excluded him from certain conversations or passed him off with a simple, "You wouldn't understand, Hack."

But Hack managed to carry his own weight at any job and he performed his job as well as he could. Most things he did as well as any other man. When he didn't perform a task right he kept trying. The same held true with life. He kept trying. And so he continued living his life exactly as he always had, trying to avoid Marjorie and her father, and all of the pretty young women he met, he simply avoided them. Sometimes men tried to taunt him into fights, this had been the way all of his life, but he was always able to convince them to leave him alone. Sometimes his size was enough of a deterrent when he stood up. Sometimes it was his silence, his unflinching stare. But for the most part he avoided conflict. When he was younger, he had knocked a few boys to the ground when they pushed him to his limits, but one thing was for sure, when he knocked them down they didn't jump back up to fight, they would lay there looking up at him with utter shock. And when he stepped over them to walk away, he would always ask, "Why did you go and make me hit you like that?" Shouting back over his shoulder to everyone around, "Just leave me alone!!!"

How he wished everyone would leave him alone. Inside his own thoughts he reckoned he would be just fine without anyone in his life. But when his mother finally passed away, Hack was thirty two years old. He had never left home. He had never had a real girlfriend. He had never known life any other way, without his mother and their small farm. When many of the townspeople attended her funeral services they were kind to Hack. They were too kind. And he couldn't look any of them in the eye. Their words of sympathy and kindness seemed artificial. He just wanted the services to end and he wanted to go home.

But home never felt the same. He busied himself as he always did. But his mind never stopped reminding him that he was imperfect. That his life was imperfect, that he would never have what others had.

It seemed he accepted this as a part of his cross to bear. When he had a job he was away from the home eight to ten hours a day. And when he got home there were many things that needed to be done. He didn't cook a single meal, his mother had always done that. But he made plenty of cold cut sandwiches and he ate at the bar with a few of his coworkers. Still, he lost weight. At first most people didn't notice. But soon enough his clothes were practically hanging from his frame.

Gertrude was the first to approach Hack about his weight loss. She was worried about him, she and Mildred had been friends since they were young mothers and she had known Hack since he was a small boy, so she asked Hack what he had been eating.

"I make ham or turkey sandwiches or baloney sandwiches most of the time."

"Can't you cook, Hack?" Gertrude asked in alarm.

"I can boil eggs, I eat boiled eggs every morning. I still have 4 hens."

"This just can't be!" Gertrude exclaimed. "Hack, you need to get back in church. We have dinners after every Sunday service and sometimes in between. And I can bring you a meal or two to the church house. You haven't been to church in two years. The Lord will see you fed either way, but I bet you will get more from life if you get back in church."

Hack agreed, and slowly he began to gain weight. He didn't miss a church service, or meal, and two of the older women carried soups, casseroles or chili to the church house every Sunday, just for Hack.

But there was a new face at the church, her name was Lily, she was close to Hack's age. And she silently observed how the two older women doted over this quiet man. Lily had moved to Brockville less than a year prior, she was the new elementary school principle. She had thick, wavy auburn hair just grazing the tops of her shoulders and she wore pretty dresses which fit tightly to her waist, yet covered every inch of her bodice and flared at the hips, ending just past her knees. She was something different indeed, so unlike all of the other ladies.

She inquired about Hack and the older women delighted in filling her in about his life. Her solution was to teach him to cook. "He has already lost his mother, and what will happen when he loses the two of you?"

Some good deeds come undone, and others go unnoticed, yet some good deeds turn out fine, while others will turn out rotten.

Lily and Gertrude spent every Sunday evening trying to teach Hack to cook. The simple dishes, the ones that stuck to a man's ribs, such as pinto beans and mashed potatoes. It would be wrong not to point out that much to his own surprise Hack was enjoying the attention, especially from Lily. She was so kind, so pretty, so quiet, yet her eyes twinkled when she smiled and she seemed to enjoy helping him. Lily said only what needed to be said, while Gertrude rambled on and on. Still, Hack looked forward to every Sunday, especially after the church service when the cooking lessons began.

But the cooking lessons only lasted a summer and soon school was back in session and Lily wasn't as free to help. She and Gertrude had taught Hack to cook many dishes and they both felt he was ready to be completely on his own.

Lily touched his shoulder on the last Sunday evening she would visit, "Hack, I am so proud of you. Look at you filling out your shirts and pants now."

Hack beamed at her praise and actually joined her in front of a mirror to look at himself, but it wasn't his reflection that captivated him, it was her standing so near, and the two of them standing there together with a frame around their images. "Nobody has done for me what you have, Ms Lily." Hack spoke before he thought and he felt heat rise to his cheeks.

Lily smiled, "Thank you, Hack, but I didn't do this alone." And she pulled him back to the kitchen where Gertrude sat, where she heaped praise upon the older woman. Finally she turned to Hack with a sigh, "As you probably are aware, school starts back tomorrow. I will be busier than a bee." She gave a light chuckle, "And Gertrude and I believe you are all set with your cooking lessons. We are proud to say that you have graduated with honors." Another little chuckle as she grabbed her purse from the kitchen counter and helped Gertrude to her feet, "We will see you at church next Sunday, but this is it, Hack. You are a self-sufficient chef!"

Hack felt his heart sink to the pit of his stomach and he watched them leave in silence. They were extending farewell gestures but he was motionless.

Maybe Hack didn't understand why or how Lily could just walk out of his life so casually and resume being polite and cordial at church, without any obvious concern or conversation beyond general kindness. Or, maybe he *did* understand but couldn't accept the reality of the implications. Whatever the case, he found himself driving by the school where she worked, watching her walk to her car almost every day. He found himself feeling a similar resentment he had felt a decade earlier when his neighbor Marjorie did the same thing, only Marjorie had been devilish and unkind. So why was he feeling that burning resentment towards Lily? She had never been unkind. Ever. And so Hack prayed. He watched her walk to her car and he prayed for God to stop the bad feelings.

Was God listening? Or was it the devil who sent the man Hack didn't recognize who began to walk Lily to her car? Who was this man? The resentment built and Hack prayed harder.

Feeding his ravenous jealousy the unknown man began to join Lily at church. It turns out he was a teacher at the same school where she was the principle. Rumors quickly circulated they were becoming a romantic item and this enraged Hack even more. He stopped driving by the school house every evening just to watch her walk to her car, and once again he stopped going to church. No amount of prayer was quieting the turmoil inside him, especially when he saw them together. He knew it was best to stay busy and stay away.

But Lily soon noticed his absence and she inquired of Gertrude and Mary about his lack of attendance. She listened politely as the older women once again whispered about their concern for Hack Brooner. She felt partly responsible for his absence at church. She realized he had developed a crush on her, but she had tried so hard not to feed the flame and she hadn't noticed how stone cold silent Hack had become after Danny began to accompany her to church. "I think it's only right that we pay him a visit." The "we" meaning her and Danny. Her hope was that Hack would see how kind Danny could be and that he would accept him being in her life a little easier.

Danny and Lily drove out to the old farm, what was left of it, and as they approached the gravel driveway Lily saw Hack working in the field, turning the garden under as winter was fast on the heels of a shortened autumn.

"This is picturesque." Danny noted as he had never actually seen the farm before, he had heard about it. To the left the land butted up perfectly to a river's edge, to the right it expanded over a field which eventually became surrounded by mountainous hills. Aside from two trailers that were segmented off from Hack's acreage, the scene was as homey and country as it could possibly get.

"Yes it is. I don't see how he manages it all alone." Lily watched Hack as he lifted his eyes to the approaching vehicle. He stopped pushing the tiller and lifted the hat away from his dampened head and wiped at the hair sticking to his forehead. "That's Hack right there. He is quiet, maybe a little slow, but kind enough. Not overly sociable, so don't take it personally."

Danny drove the vehicle to a stop and turned the ignition off. Lily thought about asking him to let the automobile run, this visit wouldn't take long. But she decided against the request, it might appear disrespectful to leave so fast.

Hack approached them calmly. She could see that he didn't recognize the vehicle or the man driving it, not yet anyway.

When Hack realized who the couple was, he paused mid stride. A heated jolt coursed through his body and it nearly made him stand still, but he forced his feet forward, carrying a solid torso above long, strong legs.

Lily spoke first, "Hack, how nice to see that you are doing well." She and the man stopped and allowed Hack to approach them. She extended her slim hand which Hack took for one small pump and nod.

"This is my friend, Danny, you might remember him from Church." It wasn't a question, but there was a hint of uncertainty that Hack would recognize him.

"Didn't know his name." Hack's eyes moved to the other man's stare and Hack watched Danny blink repeatedly as he shook hands with a stronger man with calloused palms. Danny's hands were softer and his grip not as firm.

"His name is Dan, we call him Danny, and this is Hack Brooner. He is the nice man I told you about who Gertrude and I taught to cook. How is that going for you, Hack?" Ever the kindest woman, sweet Lily with the dancing twinkle in her eyes.

Hack looked into her eyes, his heart beating quickly with admiration, "I've been cooking for myself ever since." He patted his stomach area, indicating a round belly, but Hack's abdomen was flat and hard.

"I am so proud of you." Lily nudged Danny, "He had lost at least twenty or thirty pounds before we taught him to cook."

Hack didn't care to correct her, he had lost thirty five pounds after his mother went to be with Jesus, but at the moment he wasn't in a mood to converse with the couple, instead he quietly asked God to ease the agitation he was feeling.

"We have all noticed your absence and have missed you at church, Hack, is everything going well for you?" Lily inquired.

Hack stood silently, mostly looking at Danny, wondering what she saw in this man who barely reached his chin, whose hair was neat and combed with hairspray holding it in place in spite of a slight breeze. "Everything is fine." He finally answered.

Lily tilted her head in the mannerism of shyness, "Now what has been keeping you away all this time?"

Hack wasn't sure how to answer the inquiry. His gaze danced between Lily and the man she stood near, his silence outwardly disguising that on the inside he was begging God to let him do and say the right thing, "I guess sometimes we need a break from church." He finally said.

Lily gave a little tsk tsk sound. "Far from that, Hack, we always need our church family, where God is the head of the church he is always at the center of our hearts."

Hack heard his own snort but tried to keep the words suppressed, as he wanted to say that he had no family. Hack looked at Danny, swallowing all of the contempt he harbored, it was people just like him who said one thing to his face and other rotten things behind his back, pretending for the sake of religion to care about him.

Danny shifted his weight uneasily beneath Hack's probing stare, deciding it best to conclude this visit, "We hope you will visit church again soon." And he cupped Lily's elbow as if to lead her away.

Hack didn't expect the next words that he uttered, they came from nowhere, "I've been going to church my whole life, to one church. The same one you just invited me to." His mannerism was rushed, but for Hack that meant it was normal conversational speed, "And I don't need no outsider to invite me back into my own church."

Lily stepped closer to Hack at once, "We didn't mean it that way, Hack. I remember that the ladies explained how devout your family has always been, you were an excellent member of the church." She kept her hand held palm out at Danny's chest, hoping he would allow her to finish speaking, "You have been faithful, only missing for some time after your mother passed away, which we can understand. Grief is very hard to deal with. Someone probably should have visited you sooner than we did, I would have suggested a visit if I had known…"

"You didn't know me." No one was sure if those were words of forgiveness, acceptance or rebuttal. Not even Hack. He kept praying inwardly for the couple to leave, and praying that he would not say or do anything wrong, the agitation growing in spite of his prayers.

"You are right, I didn't know you. "Lily responded, "But I am so happy I did get to know you and we are hoping you will return to the church and your church family very soon." Lily paused, she knew one of the reasons he had stopped coming, he stopped after two weeks of her bringing Danny. She felt the desire to walk away, yet she knew she hadn't eased Hack's burden. "I am truly sorry if I had anything to do with why you didn't want to come back."

Hack dropped his eyes for the first time, his gaze directed upon the ground. She was the sole reason he had no desire to return. Hack swallowed the hard lump in his throat, "If that's all ya'all came for, then you can be on your way."

Lily felt the sadness radiating from him. What could she say? "Hack, you are a dear friend." And she placed the palm of her hand on his shoulder to comfort him. His eyes traveled to her long, slim fingers and that's when Danny snickered.

"Oh, I finally get it, I see what has happened." Both Lily and Hack's eyes darted to his smiling face. "You thought she was sweet on you when she helped you learn to cook, you had a crush on Lily, didn't you? And you thought she had a crush on you, too, until I came along." Lily nor Hack knew if Danny laughed to ease the passage of his words or if he laughed maliciously, but before he could say another word, Hack had his hands wrapped around Danny's neck, while Lily shrieked and began slapping at Hack's long arms.

Hack didn't hear her pleading with him to let Danny go, all he could hear was the laughter, like so many times before, as he lifted Danny off the ground, squeezing a bright red color into the softer man's face, he heard the voices, taunting him as they laughed at his awkwardness and stupidity, "You think that girl would ever like you?" echoed a voice from his past, "You wish you could get a girlfriend." And even the voice from Marjorie, "You would like to kiss me, wouldn't you, Hack? Ha! I wouldn't even let you kiss my ass!" All of his life, he had heard the unkind words, "You're just a retard!" and another common insult was, "Did your momma drop you on your head when you was a baby?" Since pre-school children and even a few adults had taunted him. He had felt more accepted inside the church building, he had known those folk since he could recall, and those were the kind people, the ones who didn't make him feel utterly useless. Until lately. Even his church wasn't safe from scorn and ridicule and mockery. "Why did you go a make me do this?" He asked as he stared into the watery eyes of Danny.

Danny's throat burned and went bitter tasting and his vision became fuzzy. Lily screamed and punched at Hack's broad shoulders, "Put him down! Hack don't do this!!" but Hack wasn't sure if it was her voice or his own voice that shouted, "God, please stop this!!!!!"

The rage inside of Hack suddenly lessened, and he exhaled his frustration on the suppressed breath he had been holding, his grip loosening just a little, as he envisioned the faces of his church congregation, and the face of his Pastor. The voices from his past not as loud as the memories of his church family singing in the choir, or greeting him and his mother and father for all of those years when he was younger.

Danny's face was already turning purple, bright red streaks shot through the veins in his eyes and spittle dribbled from his mouth. With each passing moment the voices quieted, until there was only silence, except for his own ragged breathing, and Hack felt the tension release completely from his grip, allowing Danny to crumple to the ground.

Lily fell upon Danny, crying and speaking to him, but Hack couldn't decipher the words. He stepped across Danny's motionless legs, looking back over his shoulder, "Why can't you just leave me alone?" he implored, but neither of them heard him.

Hack felt a calmness he had never known before, was this the answer to his prayers? This stillness that was at the center of his being? Hack entered his house, his home, where he had lived all of his life. He pulled off his work boots, took off his hat and placed it on the kitchen table. Then he washed his hands and splashed cool water on his face. He went to the recliner and sat down. Time irrelevant and lost upon the dazed shock of his actions. Watching nothing, hearing nothing, he didn't even hear the sirens when the police cars drove down his driveway, accompanied by an ambulance.

When the officers entered his home, Hack didn't hear them, he sensed them and he looked at them but they might as well have been actors in a silent film, because all he heard was peaceful quietness.

Hack didn't even feel the pain from them grabbing him by his arms and slamming him to the ground, with their knees jabbed into his lower back while they handcuffed him.

Lily watched in utter disbelief as they walked Hack to the back of the police car. She was already numb from what had happened, but to see him walk with the cops without even glancing her way, or even looking at the stretcher with Danny's body laid out on the cot as the emergency crew loaded him into the ambulance left her in utter shock.

Just before the police officer slammed the rear door closed on Hack he bent and said, "You better be thankful that fella didn't die, Hack. You better pray hard that he doesn't. Or…." He held his palm outwards on a fully extended arm and swiped it from left to right, spanning the view of the farm, "Or all this right here, this here family farm, won't be yours any more. It will be sold to pay for your legal fees and you will live the rest of your life out behind bars."

Hack's silence and unblinking stare bore the confidence from the officer, who slammed the door closed on the cruiser, the sound amplified. That's when Hack said one more silent prayer. He asked his Lord to save Danny, and to forgive him for what he had done. He wasn't sure he deserved to walk as a free man again, or if he deserved to return to the family farm, but he felt calm and unworried as the police drove him away, he knew it was all in God's hands…God had indeed answered his prayers, silencing the voices, and calming the turmoil inside. Finally Hack spoke to officer, meeting his gaze through the reflection of the rearview mirror, "Everything will be alright. I know it will be, because the Bible says so, and my pastor always said so, and my mother always told me so."

The End

About the Author:

June Poore lives in Knoxville, TN. She has 2 wonderful, adult children. No grandchildren yet, but she has a host of pets and one "grand-pup!" She is waiting for the moment when she can share her love of story-telling with her own grandchildren. In addition, she has a wonderful partner in life who has given her the space to write her books. He has even had to listen to these same stories as she often reads them aloud for his opinion.

June hopes to continue to share stories with those who love a simple, short tale! Especially ghost stories! Those are her favorites!

www.ingramcontent.com/pod-product-compliance
Lightning Source LLC
Chambersburg PA
CBHW070637130626
46555CB00006B/2580